STAY

MAGNOLIA ROBBINS

Edited by Claire Jarrett

maggieromance.com

Subscribe to my Newsletter

To T, *who spent countless hours listening to me rehash my story and made it their own. I love you and appreciate all you do for me. I don't know what I'd do without you.*

To A, *thank you for all your words of encouragement, motivating me on all the days I feel so frustrated and tired with writing. I love you.*

To my betas, *I appreciate all your words of advice and critiques for the book. It made my writing stronger and I'm glad to have had your help.*

To Claire, *I've never worked with an editor like you before. This book wouldn't be what it was without your attention to detail and the love you put into your work. Thank you so much for helping me craft such a sweet story. I can't wait to work with you in the future.*

And to all my readers, who continue to support me and my work. I love you all.

Prologue

Two years ago…

Ever since she was a little girl, Lou Pearson's father had always said that dogs had a way of finding people. She'd never really thought about it much until the day she met Caspian for the first time.

It was a chilly and stormy Christmas morning. Iron gray clouds sprawled across the sky, billowing from the west and the sun's brassy glare peeked through the haze as it drained colors from the trees and burnished several patrol cars that lined the driveway, leaving the decrepit cabin at the end tinted bronze in the faltering light.

Lou had never been afraid of a little rain or of an ominous day like today was turning out to be. As a little girl, she'd embraced the wet days, eager to put on her rain slicker and rubber boots. Out she'd go; jumping, splashing, and drinking the drops of rain as they fell into her open mouth.

When she stepped from the ancient bumblebee yellow Volkswagen Beetle, out onto the gravel drive, the air grew thick around her. The scent of the rain was dark and heady. The stillness of the scene was foreboding, and in the silence came a low crackle of thunder, swiftly followed by the pattering of tiny raindrops, as it rolled across the rooftops. For a moment, everything stopped. Even the wind held its breath. A streak of hot silvery lightning split the sky, and the downpour began.

Lou darted through the torrent, garnet red hair whipping in the wind as she ran up the pair of creaking worn wooden steps, to a sturdy looking man standing under the eve of a roof. Detective Rick Kennedy was a daunting fellow, with a thick and tall frame, the exact opposite of Lou, who was small and wiry. His large head full of black hair dusted with gray looked as though it had been drying for a little while. Hazel eyes met Lou's as she fell beside him. He was probably intimidating to someone who didn't know him. But Lou had known him a while now.

"I was wondering if you were going to show," Rick's gravelly voice teased her. By the looks of it, Lou guessed that the Portland Police Department had already entered the premises. The front door, painted a dark green, had been split off from its hinges, leaving it cockeyed and swaying a little in the stormy wind. Lou imagined the detective doing one of his Chuck Norris style roundhouse kicks, and the imagery pulled a small smile to her lips. "There's a shitload of pups in there."

The Humane Society had gotten word about the police raid earlier that morning. An old abandoned cabin that had housed a puppy mill. Supposedly, a front for a methamphetamine operation, which was how the local authorities had become involved. And whenever animals were at stake, the shelter was involved, too. Lou had been volunteering there for six years and was more often than not involved in cases like these. Even if that meant coming out on Christmas Day, when she should have been spending time with her brother and his family.

Which had made Rick and her fast friends. If a person wanted to call it that.

"Merry Christmas to you too," Lou said, smiling ironically. "Megan will be here in a minute with the van." She looked over her shoulder down the oak and pine lined street. It was desolate out there. The scenery shot a chill down Lou's spine. Just as she'd spoken the words, a white van cut the corner and turned into the driveway, the Portland Humane Society logo painted along the side. Once she'd parked between a pair of black and white Dodge Charger police cruisers, Megan hopped out of the van.

Her ash-brown, shoulder-length hair caught the wind as she hoisted a paisley umbrella into the air. Next to the giant van, Megan's short, curvy frame was swallowed up. Lou waved to her from the porch. "Merry Christmas!" Megan said, offering a friendly smile as she made her way up the steps.

"Merry Christmas," Lou replied, as Megan landed beside her.

Detective Kennedy, who was always a man of business, cleared his throat. "Shall we?"

From inside, the sounds of yelping and muffled woofs echoed around the walls. Rick ducked around the door, and the two women followed, Lou last. The smell hit her hard. One whiff, and she could tell it was something dangerous. Something she didn't want any part of. Something that was stirring up memories Lou tried desperately not to think about. Her guess was that the tip had been right, and it had been a drug bust. "This is what a meth house smells like, ladies." At that moment Rick seemed to read Lou's troubled mind.

Lou pulled her shirt up around her mouth and nose, trying to shield herself from the god-awful stench which was thick with ammonia. When she was finally able to take a good look around the living room, she saw the dogs. There were crates lining the walls, two filled with poodle and schnauzer puppies and two holding nursing female schnauzers. Hickory hardwood flooring squeaked beneath Lou's black leather Bates boots, muffled by a dingy looking rag rug.

Detective Kennedy led Lou and Megan past a saggy navy-blue couch and an old-school console television. Then through the bedrooms, which were sparsely furnished. There weren't enough personal belongings to call this place a home, by any means. A wagon-wheel lamp cast a yellow glow through a grubby looking shade. In the bathroom, a poodle slept in the tub, curled up and snoring. Megan took the initiative, approaching slowly. The black ball of fur peeked through half-opened eyes, then drifted off again, uninterested.

Very un-dog like.

Lou wondered if the dog was groggy from the fumes. It was hard not to breathe them in. They permeated the entire house.

"I'll take care of her," Megan said. "And the dogs in the crates."

Lou and Rick left her to continue onward. The rest of the house seemed clear. All the dogs were contained in crates so there wouldn't be trouble hauling the animals out to the van outside, especially as they had help from the police officers on site.

Just as the pair had made it onto the linoleum floor of the 1970s-era orange kitchen, the rear door creaked. A bark drifted in from outside, stopping both of them in their tracks. Lou caught Rick's hand reaching for the Glock at his waist and waved a hand to pause him.

"Do you have the catchpole handy?" Lou asked. Detective Kennedy walked back into the living room and returned wielding a long black pole with a rope noose at the end. Lou took it from him, carefully. "You want to open the door? I'll stand here."

Rick paused, then shook his head. He made his way around Lou to the back door. "If shit gets out of hand, Lou…I won't hesitate to shoot."

"Just let me handle it," Lou replied, a clammy hand wrapped around the catchpole. Rick gave the door a yank and it flew open. A big scruffy black dog shot out, toppling over a chair in front of Lou. The animal darted past until the tether it was bolted to went taut, quivering with tension, pulling the dog to a harsh stop until it lay cowering only inches from the door.

Blocking the exit.

A low growl gave Lou warning that it wasn't happy. Not by a longshot. The dog snarled louder, teeth bared as it flattened to the floor, pulling at the restraint that wouldn't survive another serious lunge.

Even a regular Joe with no animal rescue experience could have guessed the dog was clearly freaked out and terrified, ears back, eyes wide, drool dripping from its mouth. A scared dog could be every bit as dangerous as an aggressive one.

Much like people.

"Kennedy," Lou kept her voice soft and low-pitched, securing her grip on the pole. "Keep your eyes averted from the dog until I loop the catchpole around its head."

Lou monitored the black dog out of the corner of her eye, cataloging details about the animal. Sometimes her OCD came in handy. The dog was trembling, jittery, likely from living in such a disgusting place, exposed to these god-awful fumes. She took another step, assessing, inching warily until she was finally close enough. Slipping the loop at the end of the pole over the dog's head would require finesse.

The mutt lurched toward the door, away from the cop. The bolt on the floor loosened under the strain, and Kennedy's hand twitched just over his gun. Lou winced. Shooting the animal would be a last resort, one she prayed wouldn't happen. She couldn't stomach the thought that this was the only life the poor dog would know. She had to give him a chance.

Lou took another step, extending her arm. The loop at the end was almost…

Another lunge toward the pair, and Lou heard the snapping of the chain as it broke free from the bolt. Her life flashed before her eyes in one terrifying moment, just as a blur of white filled her peripheral vision.

A large white German Shepherd appeared from nowhere, pinning the black mutt to the floor in one swift motion. Lou reacted in a split second; hands wrapped shakily around the catchpole. She tightened the loop until it was secure. The pole gave her distance from the dog for now. A sigh of relief shuddered through her, and she allowed herself an instant to breathe.

"Hey, Lou?" Kennedy said, without moving. "How about getting some more help before that beast knocks you over?"

"No need," Megan said from the doorway of the kitchen. Lou turned back to look at her. She ducked into the room, pulling a capped syringe from her pocket. She tugged off the cover and tucked the needle in the black mutt's left haunch before Lou could think.

Megan stepped back fast. "That should kick in soon and make him easier to handle." She took the catchpole from Lou. "I've got him now." Lou guessed she could sense her heightened state and breathed a sigh of relief before stepping away.

Lou stumbled into the living room, through the front door, gasping in the crisp early morning air and fighting off the crushing pain in her chest. She wiped a trickle of cool sweat from her forehead with trembling fingers, doing everything to clear away the jumble of too many emotions and sensations that were intensified so much during the holidays. Everything tangled up inside until even the good was overshadowed by the bad.

There wasn't a day that went by that she didn't think about it. But being here, in this house, amongst all these poor creatures that had been suffering...it made her think about her girlfriend. Her ex-girlfriend—Alice.

Lou hadn't blamed her for walking out. She would have too, given the circumstances. The drugs had changed her. Getting into drugs had been so damn cliché and it had been far too easy to score when she was a college student, afraid of disappointing her parents. And flunking out of veterinary school.

There was a seductive allure to those pills that seemed socially acceptable. They'd been prescribed by a doctor, after all. Then two, then three different doctors.

Then through other avenues.

After that, Lou deluded herself into believing she'd used to make sure her studies didn't inconvenience her girlfriend, only to lose her and so much more.

She blinked back tears. Lou didn't have the luxury or the time to indulge in a pity party. The yard was filling fast with more cops, another team from Animal Control, and the head of the Humane Society she volunteered with.

These were her friends, and outside of her brother and his family, the only 'family' of sorts she had anymore. Especially since she'd royally messed up her chance at starting her own family with Alice years ago.

Alice and Lou had planned on getting married and having children, once she'd finished veterinary school. Lou thought she'd have plenty of time to take care of her 'little problem.' Get through rehab. Graduate school had all gone to hell, and then Alice had found out. And she hadn't been able to get over it.

The only way Lou could now stay sane—stay alive—was to spend the rest of her days trying to make amends. She didn't expect forgiveness. She just wanted peace.

Lou sagged back against the cold wall of the cabin. The cool surface pressing against her was nowhere as intense as the chill spreading inside her. When she finally looked back at the front door, Kennedy was bringing out the white German Shepherd. The one that had risked its life to save her.

"Can I have him a second?" Lou asked Kennedy, who nodded at her and handed over the leash. Lou squatted down so she was at eye-level with him, giving him a once over. The dog had the most beautiful blue eyes, deep eyes with depth to them unlike Lou had ever seen in another dog. He was calm and present, and his demeanor caused her fragile mood to almost instantly settle.

Lou ran her long fingers over the top of the dog's head, and he leaned into the touch. "Thanks for helping me out there, buddy," she whispered. If the dog hadn't shown up, Lou wasn't sure what would have happened to her. Certainly nothing good. Lou watched his tail thumping on the ground, tongue hanging out of the side of his mouth. He certainly was a happy dog.

A yellow object caught her eye, underneath where the dog was sitting. She dug for it, and when Lou pulled it up to inspect it in the early morning light, she found it was a very worn copy of *The Chronicles of Narnia: The Lion, the Witch and the Wardrobe*. A book Adam, Lou's late father, had read to her as a child. Her blue eyes stared straight at the dog. "You're a good boy, Caspian." The name seemed to perfectly fit the dog. A heroic and noble character from the book. A smile broke across her face, as Caspian seemed rather taken with his new title, nudging against her leg.

He was something special, Lou knew it beyond a shadow of a doubt. And she knew too, that even now, his story was only just beginning.

Chapter One

The Persian green grass of the field had the bluish tinge Lou associated with the seaside. It was rough and shaggy, like uncombed hair, interspersed with bright yellow dandelions and meadow flowers. The grass flattened under the wind, in beautiful shimmering waves. In a fleeting moment, the sun cast Lou in crimson and bathed her in a rosy glow. Sunlight from behind the clouds filled the sky, pure scattered light, streaks of pinks, reds and oranges mingling with azure blue. Sparrows chirped an explicit background melody, perfectly in harmony with their colorful surroundings.

In the distance, a streak of white raced across the landscape. A German Shepherd, with a bright red harness wrapped around him, tail wagging in the wind as he pursued a neon green tennis ball. His lofty ears twitched, his nose wrinkled, and his big blue eyes scanned across the grass. In an instant, the dog flipped like a light switch, darting in another direction.

"Caspian," Lou called. The dog raced around in the field, his nose submerged in the lawn. "Hello, loonie. I'm over here." For six years, Lou had trained hundreds of service dogs, including Caspian, who she'd found two years ago in an abandoned cabin. He was the perfect candidate for a service dog, being both intelligent and kind.

And apparently a professional at making Lou out to be the world's biggest schmuck.

"Caspian!" Nothing.

Something was holding his attention. *Really* holding his attention. And it was making Lou more uncomfortable by the second.

He was lucky he was cute.

"CASPIAN!" Not even a head turn. *Jerk,* Lou thought. He'd stopped moving, hind leg paused in mid-air. His nose snuffled around a few times. A screeching hiss ripped through the quiet, sending a chill down Lou's spine. It was too late to react. Lou made it close enough to see the white and black fur, the rigid tail shooting straight up. The only thing she could do was watch, in sheer horror, as the skunk let out a nauseating spray in the direction of the rescue dog. Caspian yelped in surprise, while the critter took off through the brush.

The mid-afternoon breeze wafted a pungent odor of rotten cabbage mixed with sulfur in Lou's direction, which only grew stronger as the dog inched closer. While her mind begged her otherwise, she called out to him anyway. "Come here," Lou scolded, trying her best not to inhale. Caspian whined and stumbled over to her, half walking, half rolling in the grass in an attempt to remove the stench. When he drew close enough, Lou threw out a hand, keeping him at arm's length. "You stink something awful." She suppressed a gag, which morphed into a cough.

Hills that were clothed in a patchwork of jade and teal spanned the horizon. At the valley floor sat a row of green metal-roofed gazebos, their white paint worn with age, exposing the knobby pine beneath. A family collected at the farthest one, laying out a spread of food on the fir picnic table. Lou imagined she would have been able to make out the aroma of her brother's poached beer brats and hamburgers that were just coming off the grill, if it hadn't been for the industrial grade biological miasma that was currently invading her body. She felt as if she could taste the toxic chemicals in her mouth and felt their presence in her lungs.

"Sit," Lou instructed the dog, and he came to an abrupt halt. Once Caspian had settled in the grass, Lou continued until she'd reached the patio. Stephen, the oldest of the siblings, was turning forty in just a few weeks, he was a whole nine years older than Lou. He watched her as she approached. Side-by-side they looked startlingly similar, with untamed fiery red hair and bright blue eyes that had such an intensity about them they could pierce straight through a person. They also shared the same freckles across their fair-skinned cheeks. Her brother's nose creased. "Don't tell me Caspian found a skunk?"

Lou sulked, sliding down next to her niece, Rebecca and then grabbed a bun for her hotdog. "I couldn't get to him," she admitted, stabbing a fork into the meat and pulling it to her plate. She assisted her niece in retrieving a hamburger patty before she turned to look back at Caspian. The dog's tongue was dangling out of his mouth, his attention on some birds resting on a rusty iron fence nearby. From this distance, the odor wasn't as bad, but it was still noticeable.

"They say hydrogen peroxide, baking soda, and dish soap will get rid of it," Kelly's reassuring voice piped up across from Lou. A bright smile stretched across her oblong fair-skinned face, easing Lou's worry.

"Hopefully," Lou said, taking a bite of her hotdog. For years, every Memorial Day had been spent with her brother and his family at Rooster Rock Park. Between Stephen's grilled food and Kelly's coleslaw, it was one of her favorite meals of the year.

"Good thing you only have him for a few more days," Stephen grinned, sitting down next to his wife. Lou watched him dress a hamburger, smelling the char and grease mixed with the sour pickle brine and sharp tang of mustard, before she turned toward Caspian. Lately he'd been coming on more and more training outings with her in preparation for the arrival of his new owner next week. Lou could barely fathom the idea that they would only be working together for a short while longer.

"What's the little girl's name?" Kelly asked.

Lou paused and then realized her sister-in-law had been referring to the little girl adopting Caspian. "Anna." Lou had seen a picture of her. Five years old, with wispy sunflower blonde hair and hazel eyes, and the brightest smile that filled her rosy face. "She and her mom are traveling down from Seattle. I haven't spoken with them, but I've been told they are both charming."

"I want to know what you're going to do when that dog is gone," Stephen chortled. Caspian whined in the background, and Lou snagged a hot dog off the plate. She chucked it to the dog and watched as he devoured it in a matter of a second. While Caspian had lived the last two years at the training facility, he and Lou had always been attached at the hip. Far more so than she had been with any other dogs she had trained in the past.

"It's just a part of the job," Lou shrugged, though her heart was telling her otherwise. He was meant to be a service dog. She'd known it ever since they'd first met. "We'll be okay." A wave of emotions ran through her that hadn't hit her in a long time. Emotions that caused her palms to become sweaty and a nauseous sensation to develop in the pit of her stomach. Even though it was part of the job, it always got to Lou when the dogs went to live with their new owners. And for some reason, Caspian's impending departure was hitting her harder than most.

"I'll be back in a sec," Lou said, pulling herself up from the table.

"Where are you going?" Stephen called after her, but Lou trekked forward, heading in the direction of the parking lot. When she reached her eye-catching yellow Volkswagen Beetle, she leaned back against the door, sucking in a deep breath of air. Lou's hands dug through the pockets of her jeans, searching for something that wasn't there. Something she hadn't needed in years. When she couldn't find it, she reached for her cellphone.

Lou dialed the number as quickly as she could. The moment there was a human on the other end of the line, she sensed her body relax a little.

"Can we meet?"

T he soft flowing river glistened golden from the sunlight above, winding its way between the banks that were a vivid lush green that only summer, and Portland's rains, could bring. In the early evening light, a few hours after Lou had left Rooster Rock, the water sparkled less than it had at noon and instead it was rather mellow. The bridge that Lou always waited on, north of the city, was basic and functional. Beams of wood from bank to bank, with a rail on each side. Already, Lou was scanning the bank for rocks. Long flat rocks. The kind her father taught her to use. In her mind, she could see the two of them searching together like they had years ago.

Lou found a perfect stone and tossed it into her hand, feeling the smooth texture that had formed from its life in the water. She let it sit there for a moment, scanning the glass-smooth surface of the river. After a deep breath of crisp forest air, she chucked the rock with a slight spin out into the water. It bounced. Once, twice…three times before it disappeared from sight.

Not the best throw but satisfying none-the-less.

From behind her, Lou heard the crunching of rubber tires on the gravel parking lot. She turned, just as the ignition of a black SUV silenced. A tall, slender man hopped from the vehicle, his salt-and-pepper hair tousled by the valley breeze. Even for the cusp of summer, it got a little chilly this time of day. He hugged his brown leather jacket as he shut the car door.

Walter Harris' clear green eyes glistened in the sunlight as he approached her. There was a soft smile to his lips. He had a bit of a limp when he walked, from an injury he'd suffered during his second tour in Iraq three decades prior, and a deep rasp in his voice when he spoke from years of smoking cigars. Lou had watched him age over the years they had known each other, but he still managed to get along as best he could.

"You'd better have a good excuse for keeping me from my

supper, girl," Walt said once he'd reached her at the path between the bridge and the parking lot. "If you invited me out here just to toss damn rocks in the river…"

Lou laughed, knowing full well that her good friend had been joking, but she humored him anyway. "I thought it was about time you learned how to skip a few, Walty."

Walt's smile widened into a full-on grin. "Only you would think rocks were entertainment." He leaned into the railing on the bridge. There was something about his eyes that hinted he might not have been in great health in that moment, but Lou didn't press him. When he spoke again, his voice cut through the quiet evening air like a sharp knife, drawing Lou's attention back. "What's going on?"

"Just needed some company," Lou replied. A cryptic response, but she sensed her friend would understand. "I didn't feel like a meeting today was all."

The old man's brow raised a fraction. Still, he didn't press her. Walter knew her well enough to know she could make up her own mind.

This was precautionary. Just a cut that needed a Band-Aid. She was tough. These sorts of things she could handle.

Walter looked out at the river and Lou's gaze followed the same path. Puffs of clouds scattered across a sky that was darkening as the sun disappeared. In the valley between the hills and mountains, daylight disappeared quicker than in the city. Still, they had time.

"I gotta tell you what happened to me last week," Walt mused. The two, who used to talk daily, years ago, now spoke every week or two, depending on how busy they got. Walter and Lou had known each other for eight years now. Ever since Lou went to her first Narcotics Anonymous meeting. They were drawn to one another, sharing the same carefree attitude and quick-witted sense of humor. In desperate need of a companion, being each other's sponsors came naturally.

"What happened to you last week?" Lou asked, though she continued watching the river as a large bird hovered nearby, hunting for its dinner. A falcon, if she had to take a guess.

"I grew a pair and asked Betty to stay at my place," Walt bragged. "You know it's funny. I spent all those years snipin' in the sand, and I can't even ask a pretty lady to move in with me."

"Good for you," Lou said, glancing in his direction. The first real smile she'd had all afternoon breached her face. "What did she say?"

"Said it was 'about damn time,'" Walter laughed. Lou joined in beside him and squeezed his shoulder. They weren't the types to show too much physical affection toward one another, but Lou had the urge to change that today. Like she needed the contact. Like it would somehow erase the fact that in a few short days she'd be alone again.

"What about you?" Walter asked, the question she'd hoped he wouldn't. A lump formed in her throat. "Did you call that girl from your shelter?"

Lou shook her head. It had been two weeks now since the woman had come in. Lou had been working her afternoon volunteer shift at the Humane Society and helped her find a small Chihuahua mix to adopt. The woman was gorgeous, and Lou could tell they'd been flirting. Hard. The woman had even left her number scrawled on the adoption forms she'd filled out. Lou had meant to call her, but as usual, something had stopped her from trying. She was just too busy now, between work and volunteering and caring for Caspian.

Except she'd lose him soon. In a few weeks he'd be someone else's responsibility.

Lou tried desperately to focus on something else, her attention turning back to Walter. "I haven't had the chance to yet. I've been a little preoccupied with work."

There was a hint of disappointment in Walt's eyes, maybe even a bit of concern, but he didn't argue with her. Instead they spent a few minutes in silence, before Lou uttered her thoughts out loud. "Caspian's new owners are arriving in a few days." She glanced over at Walter, who'd turned to look at her. "I don't know what I'll do without him."

While it was hard for Lou to be honest with most people, she found it easy to open up to Walter when she needed to. He'd always been a great listener.

"I thought it was a good idea to train him to be a service animal. He's going to make a great service dog," Lou continued. "He has the perfect temperament for it." Her hand squeezed the railing of the bridge until her knuckles went white. "But I'm thinking I made a mistake. For some reason it's making me feel more alone than I've felt in a long time. Maybe I should have kept him for myself?"

Lou leaned down to grab another long thin rock from the ground and chucked it into the water. It skipped four times and the satisfaction that she'd made a better toss eased Lou's mind a little. Walter's wrinkled hand found hers, wrapped around the railing of the bridge.

"You made the right decision," Walter said, nudging her in the side. Lou did her best to concentrate on what he was saying. "And, kid. You're never alone. You hear me?"

Lou's mouth twisted upward, as she pulled a piece of wavy red hair back behind her ear. "I hear you."

Even with his words of comfort, Lou sensed a hollowness inside of her that she couldn't shake. She didn't get attached like this. Working with animals in shelters and training facilities, the animals were in and out of her life so fast, sometimes she could hardly blink.

"You sure you don't need a meeting?" Walt checked.

"I just needed some company for a few minutes. Go eat your dinner."

The pair made it up the small sloping hill to the gravel parking lot and stood between their cars. Concern clouded Walter's features. "You'll call me if you need me?"

"Of course," Lou said, nodding. Walt made his way over to the driver's side of his car, pulling open the door before Lou spoke again. "Take your lady out someplace nice, Walty. Nothing cheap. Wine and dine her."

Walt grinned. "Don't you worry, I have a good place in mind." Lou smiled and lugged open the door to her car. Just as she was about to hop inside, she heard Walt call out to her. "Oh, and Lou."

"Yeah?" She turned her head over her shoulder to look at him.
"Stop calling me fuckin' Walty."

Chapter Two

The ancient mullioned windows set the dark myrtle wood flooring of the classroom ablaze with a checkerboard of noon sunlight. A melody of pencil scratches and scuffing of erasers were the only noises, outside of an occasional cough or a sneaker squeaking across the floor. Alice Gray's eyes skimmed the room of high school students, submerged in their final examinations. Not a single head was looking elsewhere.

While she watched, Alice imagined the warmth of the early summer morning all around her. What she wouldn't have given to be walking through Pike Place Market right then, or admiring the tides as they rolled in along the coastline, or better still sipping on an iced latte from the little coffee place across from Victor Steinbeck Park. Though, if Alice needed to pick a second favorite place to be, it would be at Fremont High, presiding over her students.

She felt crestfallen to see the semester over. This final class of the semester, the final examination, marked the transition for most of her students from their life as high school kids, to college adults.

This year was a particularly eccentric group. Granted, every kid wasn't thrilled about studying Hamlet feigning madness, the pilgrimage of Odysseus, or how Virgil led Dante through the seven levels of Hell. But this semester, most of her kids had loved trying to formulate their own interpretations to Kafka's *Metamorphosis* and had even attempted to comprehend the depths of Atticus Finch. She felt crestfallen to see the semester over.

A young man walked up to Alice's desk, wielding a paper examination. While it was standard to give digital examinations nowadays, Alice still found delight in giving her student's handwritten assignments. Joey Peterson reached Alice's desk, brushing a strand of dark brown hair from his eyes before he slid the exam across to her. Once he'd sized her up and down, he glanced over to the opposite end of the desk. Sitting in an oak chair, wispy blonde hair in disarray and busy running her hands over the pages of a braille book, was Alice's only daughter. Anna had been born prematurely with malformed ocular nerves, a condition which resulted in her having a limited field of vision. While she could still make out shapes and colors, she often needed assistance with smaller and more detailed things. Still, reading braille books was one of her favorite things.

Joey squatted down beside Anna, speaking in a whisper. "What'cha reading, kid?" Her daughter's face broke into a broad smile, recognizing the voice. Most teachers didn't bring their children to school, but Anna wasn't due to attend kindergarten until the fall. The high school had made an exception for Alice, who had always been well loved there.

"It's about sea turtles," Anna explained. "Did you know that sea turtles live as long as people?" Her voice piped up in fascination. Joey grinned at Alice. The kid's smile was charming, genuine and full of charisma.

"Wow," Joey mused. "That's old, huh?" Anna's smile widened. "I just wanted one last high five before I left." Anna raised her hand up in front of her and Joey gave it a soft smack. Anna giggled, as Joey got back up to his feet. He returned to stand in front of Alice, a daunting six foot, and five inches tall. He'd been a star basketball player since he was a freshman. "Thanks for everything, Ms. Gray."

Alice studied him, holding back her emotions as best she could.

She couldn't help herself and got to her feet, making her way around the desk to give him a hug.

"You were my favorite teacher, I hope you know that," Joey said, hugging her back. Once he'd broken free, he slid his backpack up on his shoulder and turned, heading out of the room. He paused halfway, spinning back to look at her. "And good luck with the new dog."

The new dog.

Across the room at her desk, Alice saw the watercolor floral wall calendar dangling on the wall. She'd bought it a year ago after finding out they were getting the service animal. The cheerful purple Sharpie X's across each day were now drawing so close to the circled date that Alice couldn't believe it.

Her focus drew back on the rest of the students in the silent classroom, still working. She was pleased that she'd had such a good semester. Grateful, too, that it was ending. Her students were moving onto bigger and better things, but so was she.

⸻

The bench was typical of the park, the rosy cedar browns married to the iron that curved upward into arms. It was coming to resemble driftwood after years of being exposed to the elements. Alice ran her fingers over the swirls in the wood grain, lost in thought.

"Do you think it's helping?" A soft-spoken voice broke the silence. Alice's attention drifted upward until she'd met the gentle pecan colored eyes of a fresh-faced auburn haired man. He draped his hand across the back of the bench, and stared outward, toward a row of picnic tables in the distance. At the far end, Anna sat with a striking young brunette, working in a thick green notebook. The woman, Lauren, had been tutoring Alice's daughter in prekindergarten schoolwork for the past few months, meeting at a park near Alice's high school.

Alice turned her attention back to the man, still focused on Anna. Alice admired the side of his face and the softness in his eyes as Jeremy watched his daughter. There was no question how much he loved her. From the moment she'd come into the world, he'd embraced her. He'd have done anything for her. And for Alice too, for those four and a half years they'd been together.

Sometimes, Alice missed him.

"I think so," Alice confirmed. "They seem to get along."

"I was getting worried," Jeremy confessed. "But she seems okay. I'm proud of her."

"I know you are," Alice replied, wrapping her hand around Jeremy's arm and giving it a gentle squeeze. The breeze rustled through Alice's blonde hair, tousling it. She combed through the wayward strands, while she thought about catching the plane to Portland in a few hours.

Jeremy seemed to read her mind. "Excited about the dog?"

"Nervous," Alice admitted. "I feel like everything is changing a little too fast for my liking." Alice meant it in more ways than one.

It was a year now, since their divorce, but the wound still seemed fresh to her. While it had been amicable, and certainly the right decision, it hadn't been the easiest thing in the world. Somehow, they'd stayed friends through all of it. Jeremy had understood her reasons, even if it was the last thing he had wanted to happen.

Alice turned her attention back to Jeremy, whose facial expression had dropped and was now unreadable. The stirring it was giving Alice's stomach terrified her. "I need to talk to you about something," Jeremy began, his voice calm and serious. Alice sat up straighter on the bench, twisting her body so she was facing him head on. "And I'm not sure how you will react, so I'm just going to come out and say it." He paused.

It must have been the longest few seconds of Alice's life, as she sat rigid on the bench, terrified of what was about to come out of his mouth.

"I've started seeing someone," Jeremy admitted, his voice still quiet, as if worried someone might overhear him. "It's starting to get a little serious. I didn't want to tell you until I was certain it was something."

There was a terrible ringing in Alice's ears. She blinked and shook her head, trying to relieve herself of the piercing sound. A million thoughts were shooting through her mind all at once, and she couldn't sort them out. So, she sat in silence for a long while, until everything started to settle down, and the only thing left was a small painful ache in her chest. She struggled to find the words to speak. "I—I'm happy for you." Alice forced the best smile she could muster.

"You don't look thrilled," Jeremy noted, his brows furrowing with concern.

A sigh escaped Alice as she glanced over to her daughter again. "I am happy…" Her voice tapered off. "I am. I just…I think this is a painful reminder of the fact that I'm still alone."

Alice's ex-husband wrapped a reassuring arm around her shoulders. "You aren't alone, Alice," he reminded her. "And you'll find someone. You've been sorting through a lot these past few years. You needed time to understand yourself. Just be patient."

Sorting through a lot was an understatement, if there ever was one. But Alice knew she'd made the right decision, even if it hurt in that moment. She and Jeremy were friends and co-parents. That's all they'd ever be. "I'm still figuring myself out," she stated.

"And that's okay," Jeremy reminded her. Before Alice could reply, Lauren approached, walking alongside Anna and holding her hand. Jeremy got up to meet her, breaking into a smile. "Did you have fun with Lauren?"

"She was telling me all about Caspian," Lauren said, laughing. "I think she's just a little bit excited." Jeremy rested his hands on Anna's shoulders. They chatted for a minute, but Alice couldn't tell what they were saying. She was still sitting on the bench, unable to stand, a hollow ache in her chest that wouldn't stop.

Alice knew she'd made the right decision. She knew without any doubt. But it still hurt. There were still days where everything was a painful reminder of the consequences of her actions. Jeremy was moving on, when she wanted so desperately to be moving on too. To not be stuck in this limbo she'd been in for years. While she and Jeremy would always remain good friends, Alice knew they'd never be partners. Not in the way he wanted, anyway. She'd known that for a long time now, but had been in denial about it until the previous year.

"Are we going now?" Anna asked. Alice forced herself up from the bench and reached for her daughter's hand, squeezing it. Jeremy was right. She wasn't alone. There was Anna. And soon there would be Caspian too.

Jeremy laughed. "All right, kiddo. Let's get you guys to the airport."

"Thanks, Lauren," Alice smiled at her, as Anna began walking down the sidewalk, tugging her along. She looked back over her shoulder, waving with her free hand. "See you in a few weeks."

"Good luck," Lauren called back as they hustled down the sidewalk.

Luck, Alice thought. She could use a bit of that nowadays.

The car radio played notes of a familiar classical melody, the strings gliding into the last few measures of the song. When it concluded, the host of the show came on a few seconds after. *"That was Moonlight Sonata, by Ludwig van Beethoven. Performed by the New York Philharmonic with solos by Juliet Hamilton, Miranda Kepner, and new member Emma Harvey. Next up we have the St. Louis Symphony performing Vivaldi's Four Seasons."*

Alice's attention was drawn to the window as the city lights of downtown Portland whizzed by her. It seemed somewhat like a mirage, having been awhile since she'd last visited. A fact her father pointed out as they pulled to a stop at a red light. "It's about time you came home," James said, breaking Alice's train of thought. "A year is a long time." Her focus turned to her mother Lily, who was playing with Anna in the car's backseat.

"I'm glad to be back," Alice replied. While she loved Seattle, there was something about her hometown that was comforting. Even if it came with painful memories. Alice loved Portland, and all of its charms.

"We've got a pot roast in the slow cooker for dinner," Lily said. "I hope that's okay."

"I love roast," Anna piped up, and the car erupted in laughter.

"Grandma made it just for you," Lily replied, pinching her cheeks. Anna squealed, and Alice leaned back in her seat. It was nice to be back in the company of her family. The loneliness had been dreadful after her divorce. Perhaps this is what she'd been missing.

"How was the last day of school?" James asked, pulling onto the familiar streets of Arlington Heights. A row of Craftsman and bungalow-style houses stretched as far as you could see, with bigleaf maples lining the sidewalks. Alice rolled down the window, smelling the cool evening air and dewy leaves as they caught the breeze.

Alice rambled on about her students for a few minutes. It was the same mundane conversations with her parents every time. "I have to grade finals while I'm here, but I'm confident most of them did well. They were a good group."

Teaching had been something that Alice knew she'd pursue from a young age. A family tradition. Both her mother and her grandmother taught for many years, so it seemed only natural for her to follow in their footsteps. It was the safe choice.

Lily piped up from the backseat as they turned again. "And how is Jeremy? He hasn't called in a while. Is he still enjoying his new job?"

It was another question that was often brought up when they spoke. Alice couldn't blame them; Jeremy was rather attached to her family. "I think he's enjoying it a lot. It keeps him busy." Like Alice, Jeremy had majored in teaching, which had been where they'd first met. They'd bonded quickly as friends, and after the nasty breakup Alice had experienced in graduate school, he'd been the raft that had kept her from drowning in her own self-pity. And while she'd never expected to marry a man, they'd both wanted children and a family, so at the time it had felt like the right thing to do.

Alice looked back at her daughter, Anna was sleeping, her stuffed turtle in her lap. The car was quiet for a few minutes, before Alice's mother spoke again. "I miss Jeremy," she whispered, and

Alice knew that she would not like what followed. It wasn't the first time Lily started this conversation. "I don't understand why you two couldn't work things out."

"Lily…" James warned, but Alice's insides were already churning.

"We're not getting back together." Alice was firm in her reminder. She kept her voice calm and soft, so as not to disturb her daughter. "I've told you this a dozen times."

"It just seems like you both get along so well. Don't you think it would be good for Anna?" Alice had heard all these arguments many times before, but they still struck a chord every time. She tried her best to be patient and understanding. They didn't get it, and she couldn't expect them to.

"You're right, we do get along well," Alice agreed. "And we're doing our best to co-parent, given the circumstances. But we have our reasons. Sometimes relationships just don't work." Truthfully, Alice was the deciding factor for the divorce.

"I just think it's a mistake," Lily muttered from the backseat.

"Mom…" Alice warned, feeling her blood pressure rising in the form of an intense throbbing between her eyes. She rubbed her pulsing brow, trying to soothe the headache that was starting to brew. "We're adults. I think we can make these sorts of decisions ourselves." She looked at her father, who was focused straight ahead. It was clear he was doing his best to stay out of it. Alice only wished her mother would come to the same conclusion.

"Sweetheart," Lily said calmly and quietly, so as not to disturb Anna. "You both have to think of your daughter."

"Jeremy has nothing to do with this," Alice had lost her train of thought, feeling her blood boiling and her body exploding all at once. "It was me, Mom. I don't feel that way about Jeremy anymore. It was me. I just wasn't happy." Ever since she'd graduated college, Alice's parents had been pressuring her into getting married and having children. And, as much as she would never regret having Anna, she felt she'd made a brash decision ever since she'd married Jeremy. Like she'd done everything important in her life for the wrong reasons, just to appease her family. Who had never been unsupportive of her sexuality in high school and college but had always hinted that they would prefer she marry a man and have kids. "I'm sorry if I've disappointed you."

Lily opened her mouth to argue again, but the car had made a final turn into a white paved driveway. "We're here," James blurted, as Alice unbuckled her seatbelt in a fury. Never more grateful to get out of a car in her life.

Chapter Three

Lou had always loved animals. Ever since she was a little kid. When she was five, just after her mother had passed away, Lou's father Adam had found a Pointer mix behind a dumpster in downtown Portland and had brought it home. It had crazy curly gray and white hair and a sharp face and Lou and Stephen had called the dog Benji. Benji had been Lou's everything for twelve years, until she'd started high school. When the dog had gotten bone cancer and passed away, Lou had sworn she'd go to college to become a veterinarian. That she'd save other dogs from the fate hers had suffered.

But plans changed.

When she met Megan Hannaford, of the Portland Humane Society, at a Narcotics Anonymous meeting, shortly after Alice had left and she'd dropped out of graduate school, volunteering at the animal shelter had seemed like the perfect way to occupy her time. Helping animals that couldn't advocate for themselves.

Then Tammy Bard had come along. Beautiful Tammy, with her thick curly black hair and silky brown skin. The woman with the killer smile that had fallen in love with a rescued Goldendoodle at the shelter that she'd since named 'Noodles'. She'd told Lou she had a way with animals. Explained how she was opening a new facility just outside of Portland, to help train guide dogs. And even when Lou had been honest about her past, the woman had been understanding. Tammy believed what Lou hadn't back then. That she was meant for the job and deserved to be given a chance. That she had found her calling, even more than her dream of becoming a veterinarian.

And now, Lou couldn't have imagined doing anything else.

P erfect spheres of rainbow-colored soap bubbles swirled and danced along the alabaster ceramic tile flooring of one of the empty dog kennels in the back of the Portland Guide Dog Association building, just outside of Troutdale, Oregon. Lou spent most of her days there, doing everything from training new dogs and working with their owners, to cleaning kennels and washing the dogs. She was busy finishing up the last of the floors when she heard the familiar bark down the row.

"Alright, Caspian," Lou called out to him, stowing the mop once she'd finished wiping the floor clean. "I'm coming."

The tall and lean, snow-white German Shepherd, with the dazzling blue eyes, moseyed out to the center of the training room, looking relieved to be finally able to stretch his legs outside the confines of his kennel. He waited, tail thumping against the tile, his tongue rolling out of the side of his mouth. Lou slid a red halter over his head and shoulders, padded with straps that fastened around his lower neck and behind his front legs. On either side, a navy-blue patch with white lettering read, 'WORKING DOG – DO NOT PET', and across the back, it declared, 'SERVICE ANIMAL'.

"Good boy, Caspian," Lou said once she'd secured the halter. After a scratch on top of his head, she fed him a handful of treats. "You ready to work?" The dog gave a small, affectionate bark, before Lou wrapped his black leash in her hand. "Heel."

The putrid stench of the skunk hadn't worn off. Every so often Lou got a whiff. Even still, he smelled better than he had days prior.

Tolerable enough, since today was the first day of training with his new owner.

"Sit." Lou paused, giving the hand signal, fingers raised above his head. Caspian sat next to her and Lou handed off more treats. "Great job, buddy. Other side." Lou waited as Caspian paused, watched her walk a pace ahead, and then changed to walk on her right side instead of her left. "Good boy."

An excited chorus of barks sounded from across the room. Lou didn't even have to look to know who it was. Two other Labrador Retrievers joined Lou and Caspian in the training room, along with their trainers, preparing for the orientation. Tammy peeked her head around the corner last, toting a black lab beside her.

"Good. You're all here." Tammy rounded the corner with the final Labrador Retriever of the group. All three, and Caspian, would meet their new owners today. "We've got parents and kiddos coming any minute now. Everybody doing okay?" The group nodded, even Lou whose stomach was tied in knots in its usual fashion. She did her best to ignore it, stroking the top of Caspian's head. When the front door squeaked open, all heads turned.

A wiry young girl with wispy, sunflower blonde hair darted into the room with her walking cane in front of her. She was only five, but she moved like a bullet, running speedily ahead of her mother.

"Wait for me, Anna." A sweet, soft-mannered voice echoed outside the door, distinctive even over the sounds of the other people that had gathered inside. The sound lifted Lou to a place where she assumed she was dreaming, as if her soul had left her body. It was a sound that she recognized the instant she heard it but she was still not sure if her ears had deceived her.

The moment Alice Gray turned the corner into the building, Lou's entire world stopped. She stared in disbelief, sure that the woman standing before her wasn't real. That she was dreaming.

Alice still looked almost the same, only with her thick blonde hair cut short, and her bangs swept across her head. A broad, warm smile lit up the entire length of her face. Lou would never forget that smile. Even if it had been eight years since she'd last seen it.

Lou stood frozen in space. Unable to move. Unable to breathe.

Instead, she watched Alice's mesmerizing eyes of hazel and honey, shining like sunlight on polished stone, scan across the room in slow motion.

Lou's heart was threatening to rip straight from her body, racing at full speed. A wave of nausea rippled through her, and cold sweat was dripping down her face like she'd been doused with a bucket of ice water.

It felt like she was dying.

"Get out!" Lou heard Alice screaming at her in her mind like they were breaking up again that very moment. The memory was like a fresh wound, cutting through her.

The second her legs wobbled, Lou raced from the room. She left Caspian where he was, not giving Alice an opportunity to see she was there, and quickly scrambled to get behind closed doors, where she'd be alone. She grasped at her chest, the pain inside her unbearable. As soon as the door shut behind her, Lou collapsed to the floor, fighting to suck in air.

She would not make it through this. This was it. The time that her past would kill her. Lou knew her heart was about to explode into a thousand pieces, and there was nothing to stop it. Instead, she lay helpless on the floor, whimpering and with soundless tears streaming down her face, unable to move or think.

Her hands fumbled through her pockets. Of all the times she'd ever needed a fix, there wasn't a more desperate time than now. Even though she knew there was nothing there to help her, not anymore. She searched anyway, pleading with the universe. Drugs had saved her so many times before. They'd kept her sanity before she'd abused them.

It hadn't occurred to her that she needed them that much. Not until this moment.

It was just over eight years ago, that warm May evening when Alice came home to find Lou sprawled out on the floor, out of her mind. *"Get out, Lou!"* All Lou recalled was the panic after her first semester graduate school finals. She'd barely made it through them. She remembered thinking in class how much she needed relief. Something to take the edge off.

It was that way for years. She'd been out of control.

"You lied to me," Alice cried as she threw Lou's things out of their two-bedroom apartment and into the hallway. Even though she was high as a kite, Lou still tried to keep up with her. Tried to make sense of what was happening. "All this time you've been lying to me. Get out! I never want to see you again."

"Alice, please," Lou begged her. "You don't understand..."

"You're an addict." Alice's voice turned hard, chilling in that moment. Like she'd finally come to that realization herself. "You're an addict, and you've been in denial for years. Just admit it." Alice had known. She'd known a long time and still stuck by her. But then Lou had started pulling away. Shutting everything out around her. Refusing to go out, shutting down at even a hint of stirring up her anxiety. She'd become a recluse, and it had clearly been the last straw for Alice, who wasn't able to help her anymore.

And what it all really boiled down to was that Lou didn't really want help.

"I can't help you if you won't let me, Lou. And I'm tired of fighting you on this anymore. So, please, just get out. I don't want to see you ever again."

"Alice, please—" Lou continued to plead with her, but her girlfriend wasn't having it. The look on Alice's face said it was over. There was nothing Lou could do.

The last images of Alice were with swollen red eyes and tears streaming down her face. The door slamming behind her as Lou fell in a disheveled heap on the hardwood floor of the hallway, her belongings piled around her.

Lou would never forget that moment. Not as long as she lived.

She gasped and struggled to take a breath. She wasn't aware of the time passing. Her mind was drifting in and out of consciousness, unable to fend for itself. Someone sat beside her on the floor, running a hand over her soft wavy hair, stroking the side of her face.

It relaxed her. Lou breathed in and out slowly until her thoughts became less hazy and she could think straight again. When she looked up, Tammy was there. There was a look of concern in her amber eyes. She was beautiful, so much that it was almost unfair. And she was one of the kindest people Lou knew, too. Not unlike Alice.

She was also one of the few people that understood Lou when she was at her worst. "What's going on? What's gotten you so upset?" Tammy asked, no judgement in her voice. Only compassion.

"I'm fine," Lou breathed, and though she'd relaxed, her body was still trembling. She tried to focus on anything else, anything besides her anxiety.

"You aren't," Tammy argued. Lou sat upright, leaning back against the dark gray walls of the building. "What do you need?"

Even though she was hesitant, and not at all certain she wanted to, Lou briefly explained her past and how shocked she had been to see Alice. When they'd first met years ago, Tammy had known some of the story, but it wasn't until that moment that she'd gone into detail. "I just need a minute," Lou replied, though she knew she needed more than a minute. She wasn't sure how she would force herself back into that room. The thought of seeing Alice again sent Lou's heart pounding. "I can't tell you how much I want some relief right now." Lou sighed. "And not an appropriate relief."

Tammy studied her, looking as if she was unsure of what to say. Her face grew stern. "Lou, you need to get it together, okay? You have a room full of people outside. A room full of people that need you right now. Can you do that for me? The minute classes are over, I'll take you to a meeting. But you need to hold it together for two hours."

Lou wasn't sure if that was possible, but she didn't see another choice. She forced herself to take in air and swallow, before slowly standing up. "Okay," she breathed, squeezing her eyes shut for a moment to fight off the dizziness that was threatening to overwhelm her.

The walk from the kennels to the doorway leading back out was lengthy. It seemed as if she was trudging through thick mud, unable to move. By the time Lou's hand reached the doorknob to the training room, it was shaking. Her breathing grew ragged and her heart was thudding against her rib cage.

Even though Tammy was now clear on what was wrong, she rested a compassionate hand against Lou's shoulder. "You will be okay, you know? Keep taking deep breaths. One foot in front of the other."

One foot in front of the other. Lou could do this. She could make it. A few long breaths escaped her before she pulled open the door and stepped out into the room, Tammy following at her heel. And for a split-second Lou felt as if she were able to take on the world. As if there wasn't a haunting piece of her past sitting only a few yards away from her.

When Lou's attention turned to Alice Gray, her world stopped. The confidence she'd felt for just a short moment dissipated into the air like it had never existed. Soft milk chocolate eyes rimmed with a deep forest green locked on her. Pierced through her like daggers. Dragged the years of guilt back to the surface like it was only yesterday.

Chapter Four

Alice studied the blue and cream trimmed building that towered in front of her. Lined with hibiscus bushes in full bloom, their pink buds added to the ambiance of the already cheerful looking landscape. Across the far side of the campus, the Columbia River swept by behind a blue-green field, filled with flowers of all shapes and sizes. The balmy summer air tousled her short blonde hair as she looked back toward the front of the building.

Anna had already disappeared inside, the door ajar. "Wait for me, Anna," she called, hustling her way in behind her. Alice's stomach was fluttering unlike anything she'd ever experienced. She was never one to get nervous, but it was different today. The place was just as vibrant inside as it was out. Shades of gray and teal blue decorated the entire length of the building. The entire room went quiet as they entered.

Across from Alice and Anna there were four dogs with trainers. Three Labrador Retrievers, and a white German Shepherd. Alice's voice got caught in her throat when she saw the dog. It was almost as if she was living a dream. She reached for Anna, placing a hand on her shoulder. "I see Caspian," she whispered. Her daughter froze in place.

Something happened, but Alice wasn't sure what. The two trainers in the room murmured to one another. A petite woman with strawberry blonde hair picked up Caspian's black leash from off the ground. She was holding on to one of the black labs, but she managed with the two dogs together. The three made their way over to Alice and her daughter, Caspian speeding ahead with a sense of abundant curiosity. Anna leaned into Alice, waiting as the dog approached.

Caspian sniffed Anna over once he'd gotten to her. Alice's daughter's small hands reached out for his face, finding it with ease. Anna broke into a smile that stretched the entire length of her face and she laughed as Caspian licked her across her cheek. A soft cry escaped Alice, placing a hand over her mouth. She was in disbelief that this was real. After a year of waiting, this day was finally happening. Their dog was here, and they were together.

"Sit, Phil," the blonde broke the silence, looking down at the Labrador beside her. The black dog sat, tail wagging behind him. "Good boy." The woman looked at Alice whose focus turned on her. "Felicity," she stretched out a hand with a smile.

"Alice," she replied, taking the woman's hand and offering it a firm shake. "It's nice to meet you and Caspian." At the mention of his name, Alice looked back down, finding her daughter engrossed in the dog. "I haven't heard much about you."

"Oh, I'm not Caspian's trainer," Felicity explained. "I'm not sure where Lou went, but I'm assuming she'll be back any moment. I just wanted you to meet your new dog."

Alice, who was simultaneously shifting her attention from the trainer to the dog, almost missed the name. When she heard it, she felt her heart take pause in her chest. *Did she just say Lou?* It couldn't be the same person. *Could it?*

A door squeaked open from across the room. Alice focused on the dog and her daughter again, both of them acting as if they'd been the best of friends for years. "Oh, there's Lou." Felicity's voice brought Alice's attention back to the present, toward the sound of the door she'd heard open.

The excitement that was coursing through Alice at the thought of her daughter with her new dog faded the moment she saw Lou.

Lou Pearson, the drummer in the marching band in high school, the cute girl drawing sketches in her notebook in the lunchroom's corner. The one in *Death Cab for Cutie* shirts and Converse sneakers, colored on with Sharpie pens. The last person on the face of the planet that Alice imagined would have been her girlfriend through her last year of high school and through college. But there she'd been, ever since they were seniors without a care in the world. Ever since they were paired together in AP Chemistry.

Her untamed flame red hair was unmistakable, the same as it was when they were attached to the hip all those years ago. The same intense dark blue eyes, like ocean pools with unbelievable depth. She just looked a little older, maybe even a little more relaxed than she used to be. But she was still the same Lou she'd known all those years ago.

The same Lou that was Alice's everything for six years. The same Lou that broke her heart to pieces. Alice's insides recoiled as she vividly recalled the long-buried memories.

It was as if the world moved in slow motion as Lou came to stand in the center of the room, alongside another woman. Alice recognized Tammy's smooth brown skin and curly ebony hair. She was the owner of the center; her face was on every brochure and on the website that Alice had scoured over for months. So, why hadn't she seen Lou in any of the pictures?

Her ex-girlfriend trailed over to join Alice and Anna. Lou's gaze would, from time-to-time, drift upward to meet Alice's, but mostly she remained focused on the dog and Anna. By the time she'd made it to them, Alice was finding it difficult to breathe.

The entire moment seemed impossible. A dream.

"You must be Anna." Lou's voice broke the silence. Just hearing it made Alice's stomach ache in ways that she never expected. Lou's voice was interesting, deeper than most women, with a scratchy quality to it. It made her discernible in a crowd.

Why on Earth, out of all the people in the universe, was Lou there? Alice didn't think it was possible she'd be able to stand being in a room with her for the four weeks of training, let alone that morning.

"I'm Lou, Caspian's trainer. Nice to meet you."

"Hi Lou," Anna was still smiling, letting the dog lick her fingers.

Alice did her best not to focus on Lou, even though there were butterflies in her stomach that were trying to escape. Somehow, she found her voice. "Anna, do you have questions about Caspian?" There were plenty of questions Alice wanted to ask. Most of them had nothing to do with the dog, so she figured she'd let her daughter do the talking.

"How old is he?" Anna asked, petting along his backside in long, soft strokes.

"He's three," Lou replied. "Makes him about twenty in human years." Caspian looked about as content as he could be, staring at Lou with loving eyes. It was clear the two were bonded.

It was hard not to bond with Lou. She was a likeable person.

Had been, Alice reminded herself. Lou had been a likeable person.

Anna's smile grew wider. "That's *old*. That's almost as old as Mama." Lou laughed, and Alice laughed right alongside her.

That sound. She hadn't realized how much she'd missed Lou's laugh until she heard it again. It was melodic to her ears. Lou's laugh was magnetic, it could drag anyone in. It was genuine and hearty and full of emotion. When she laughed, she meant it. The sound echoed in Alice's mind.

When they looked at one another again, Lou opened her mouth but was interrupted by Tammy, who appeared beside them. "You ready?" The expression on Lou's face seemed like she couldn't be *more* ready. Lou bobbed her head in confirmation and then turned her attention back to Alice.

"It was nice seeing you."

Nice seeing you.

Alice stood stunned as the former love of her life walked away with Caspian, without so much as a second glance back at her. The three trainers and Tammy gathered together. Alice realized, once she'd focused on the rest of the room again, that it had filled up with several other families.

"If everyone could just take a seat for a few minutes," Tammy ushered everyone toward the plush gray benches that lined the walls. Alice took hold of her daughter's hand and the pair made their way across the room. No matter how much Alice tried, she couldn't fight the racing thoughts in her head. Lou Pearson was just a few yards away from her. A whole state had divided them for years now, until some divine intervention had decided to bring them together again.

She would not make it. Not for four weeks, anyway.

"Where's Caspian?" Anna asked as they found a place to sit.

"He'll be back soon," Alice promised, brushing a strand of her own blonde hair out of her face. She turned her focus to a man towering beside her with a girl Alice presumed to be his daughter. He sat a few seats away, helping the little girl he was with sit down next to Anna. As soon as they'd settled, his attention turned to Alice and he flashed her a charming white-toothed smile.

The man wasted no time. "I'm Cooper." He extended his hand and Alice took it after a moment. "And this is my daughter, Jesse." Jesse's attention turned toward the sounds.

"Alice," she replied.

"I'm Anna," Alice's daughter piped up beside her. Jesse seemed a little more reserved than Anna and didn't reply. Instead, she turned her head to Anna, listening. "Are you getting a dog, too?"

"Yeah. His name is Phil," Jesse said. Alice remembered the dog with Felicity a few minutes ago, the obedient black lab. "He's one year old."

"My dog's name is Caspian," Anna replied. "He's three. That makes him twenty in human years."

"That's *old*," Jesse mused. Alice and Cooper exchanged smiles as their daughters talked.

"Do you live here?" Anna asked Jesse. "Mama and I live in Seattle."

We flew here but we're going to drive back with Caspian." Alice confirmed.

"You guys traveled quite a ways," Cooper noted, and Alice nodded in agreement. He looked out into the room, scanning the trainers and the dogs gathered in the center. "Which one's yours?" Alice followed his gaze, eyes settling on Caspian, and then back on Lou. She shook her head, turning back toward Cooper. The less she thought about Lou, the better. "Ours is the black one over there. Supposedly they all have an excellent pedigree."

"Caspian's a rescue," Alice explained. "The German Shepherd. His trainer found him a few years ago." By trainer, Alice was again referring to Lou, who she couldn't seem to get off her mind, to an almost frustrating degree. She knew, by admitting the fact that Caspian wasn't a part of the Labrador litter, that this would single her out as the one who couldn't afford a regular service animal. As a single parent on a teacher's salary, paying fifteen thousand dollars for a dog was next to impossible, even with the fundraising she'd done over the past year. "They were so generous letting us have a rescue dog instead of having to go through the regular program." Alice was rambling.

Cooper held up a hand. "You don't need to explain," he reassured her. "I get it. You do what you have to do for your kid, right?" Alice gave a shy smile and Cooper looked out into the room again. He pointed at Caspian, who was sitting beside Lou. "Is that him?" Alice bobbed her head again, and Cooper's smile grew bigger. "Pretty guy, isn't he?"

"Very," Alice agreed, though her attention was on Lou's face, admiring her features. *God, she's aged well.* She licked her lips, realizing she'd been staring for an indecent amount of time. Before Alice could dwell on it, Tammy turned her attention toward the row of parents and children waiting for her to speak.

"It looks like everyone is here, so I think we'll get started." Tammy beamed, clapping her hands together. "I'm Tammy Bard, the director and owner here at the Portland Guide Dog Association. We're glad you're here with us. I hope you've been getting to know one another, since you'll be working together for the next month."

When Alice glanced in Lou's direction, it surprised her to see her staring right back. Their gaze lingered, before both of them turned their attention back to Tammy. Alice fought every instinct to run, trying to remain collected. She could do this. She *had* to do this.

"I will let you all get to know your new companions. Our trainers will be here to guide you through introductions. Let me know if you have any questions."

Once Tammy concluded her speech, the group of trainers gathered to converse. A few times, Alice caught Lou eyeing her and wondered what the group was discussing. Before long, Felicity moved over to Cooper and Jesse. "Good luck," Cooper said, nodding at Alice before he got up to help his daughter.

Alice waited for Tammy and Lou to finish their conversation, dreading the idea that any moment Lou would come back. That somehow, they'd have to work together. Even the next hour and a half seemed daunting and that didn't include the eleven classes that were due to follow.

Expecting Lou to come over, it surprised Alice when Tammy came instead, Caspian at her side. Meanwhile, Lou took the golden lab over to a couple and their teenage son at the opposite end of the room. Alice turned her attention to Tammy. "You must be Alice Gray," Tammy said, extending a hand. Alice shook it and smiled. "Pleasure to meet you, I'm Tammy. I'll be working with you and…" Tammy squatted down so that she was at eye level with Anna. "Anna, right?" Alice's daughter nodded. Meanwhile, Caspian's nose nudged at the young girl's fingers.

Anna beamed, cupping her hands around the dog's snout. "Hi, Caspian!"

"What happened to Lou?" Alice asked, although she was relieved to see Tammy instead.

Tammy's face dropped, showing a great deal of concern in her eyes. Alice knew that Lou had told her something. Things she had no business knowing. "Lou just thought, given your circumstances, I might be a better fit to work with you and Anna."

"Given our—" Alice's gaze shot to Lou, who was busy talking on the opposite side of the room. There was a smile stretched across her face as she loved on the Labrador at her feet, along with the rest of the family. She looked totally absorbed and in her element. *Good for her*, Alice thought, somewhat bitterly. She shrugged off the sudden tinge of anger at the thought that Lou had shared their private business with Tammy.

"You ready to learn some tricks with Caspian?" Tammy asked Anna. Anna nodded, and Alice focused her attention back on her daughter. It looked like she didn't have a choice whether or not she worked with Tammy.

And for whatever reason, Alice wasn't sure how she felt about it.

When the classes ended for the day, Alice searched for Lou as her daughter said goodbyes to Caspian for the night. The fiery redhead was gone. Alice brought herself back to the room just in time to see Cooper and Jesse approaching. "How'd everything go?" Both his and his daughter's hands were firmly wrapped together. Anna made conversation with Jesse the minute she heard them approaching.

"Did you learn how to shake?" Anna blurted.

Jesse grinned, her head leaning in the direction of Anna's voice. "Yeah! And I got to throw a ball!"

"Me, too!" Anna exclaimed. Alice turned her attention back to Cooper, unable to help her lips from curling with happiness. Even with how distracted she'd been all day, she was relieved her daughter was enjoying herself so much. That she'd made friends.

"It went well," Alice said, nudging her head over to Anna. "As I'm sure you can tell."

Cooper laughed and looked over at the girls. "I think so, too," he agreed. Then he paused. "Jesse and I were wondering if you and Anna might want to go grab a bite to eat. I know you aren't from Portland, but we know some great spots. Portland is *the* place for food."

"I grew up here," Alice replied. For half a second she thought she might take him up on his offer, but after this emotionally exhausting day, she wanted nothing more than to get back to her parents' house. As far away from Troutdale as she could be. "It's sweet of you to offer, but can I take a rain check?"

Cooper nodded without a second of hesitation. He didn't look disappointed like Alice imagined he'd be. Instead, he looked rather understanding and handed her a business card. "I'll hold you to it. I know Jesse is full of questions for Anna."

The four made their way out of the building, and Alice couldn't help but do a final sweep of the room, searching for Lou, who'd disappeared. "I'm looking forward to it," Alice replied. "Have a good evening."

"Bye, Anna!" Jesse shouted over her shoulder as she and her father headed to the parking lot.

"Bye!" Anna replied, just as Alice turned her in the opposite direction toward their car. She couldn't help but take a quick look back, feeling as if she was being watched. Sure enough, at a corner window on the side of the building, a light was on. Alice could have spotted her crazy red hair from a mile away. Lou was staring straight at her, an unreadable expression on her face. A lump formed in Alice's throat.

Lou Pearson, whose pink kissable lips reminded her of happier times. Whose calming words were like a summer rain that washed away all her insecurities. Whose beseeching blue eyes stole every piece of her all those years ago. Alice studied her, frozen and helpless.

"Mama," Anna tugged on her hand and Alice's attention drew downward. "Are we going to Grandma's?"

When Alice glanced back up at the window, Lou had vanished. And in that moment, Alice realized, she was just a memory. Those days were past, never to come again.

Chapter Five

L ou stared at a large oil painting of the Descent from the Cross that hung across a chipped eggshell white wall. The edges were fading and yellow, and the tacky gilded gold frame showed more than one layer of dust caked in its corners. An aroma of stale wafer cookies and burnt out cigarettes mingled with the dankness of the basement. Lou ran her hands up the length of her naked arms, warming them from the frigid draft blowing around the room.

She shifted in the maple ladder-back chair beneath her, unable to get comfortable. The fluorescent lights flickered above, dusty and showing their age. Beside Lou, a Solo cup filled with sweet tea teetered in a wrinkled hand. Walter was making conversation with his neighbor, another veteran who was a regular. If it wasn't for the crazy day she'd had, Lou might have been more inclined to pursue conversation. Instead, she lost herself in the painting on the wall.

Above them, there were the faint sounds of a choir practice. The harpsichord rang through the thin walls blending in with the exchanges. As the room filled, with every vacant chair soon taken, latecomers slouched against the walls whilst others stood near the exits. The First Lutheran Church had housed these meetings since Lou had started coming eight years ago.

A stirring at her feet brought Lou's attention back to the room and out of her head. Caspian lay on the floor, adorned in his red service dog halter. He'd been to more than one of these gatherings in his two years of living with Lou. He seemed rather nonchalant about the whole thing, though some of the members walked up to pet him.

"Let's get started," a voice broke the noise of the crowd, and the area came to a standstill. Across from Lou, Evan Peters gave a polite wave to the room. With a voice that was as hard as the blade of a shovel, and colossal arms that were bursting with ink, he was the type of person you *didn't* want to meet in a dark alley. Evan commanded attention, but his kind, toothy smile and soft brown eyes drew you in. "We have a lot of veteranshere tonight, but I see one or two new faces. So, hey. I'm Evan, and I'm a recovering drug addict. I've been moderating these meetings for thirteen years now." Lou heard the squeak of a chair leg against the concrete floor. "There's no judgement in this room. We don't care about what drugs you've used, or how often you've used them. Just how they've impacted our lives. This isn't therapy, but it is a safe place to share."

Lou felt the need to speak creeping up on her like a kindling flame that was begging to burn out of control. This was the safe space she needed. The people that needed to hear and would understand what was on her mind. The room recited the Serenity Prayer, and then Evan glanced around. "Anybody want to start us off?" The second Evan finished asking, Lou's hand shot into the air. He inclined his head toward her, and Lou got to her feet.

"Good evening, everybody," Lou spoke to the room full of people. People who came with no preconceived judgement, but who were honest and sincere. People who wanted to get better. Some of these folks Lou had known as long as Walter. "I'm Lou, and I'm a recovering drug addict."

"Hi, Lou," various voices from around the room echoed in response.

Walter was watching from beside her and gave her an encouraging smile when their eyes met. Lou took a deep breath, sucking in the humid air of the room. "I guess I'm having a rough day," she admitted. "Someone from my past came back into my life today, and I'm not sure how I feel about it. The last time she was in my life, I hurt her badly. And now she has a family and a life outside of mine...I don't want to hurt her again. I *can't* hurt her again."

A few nodded along, most eyes focused on her. Lou was never a big fan of speaking in public, but there'd been something about these meetings. They brought a sense of relief unlike anything else in her life could bring.

"This woman...she knew me back when I was using. She left because I was using. I think she's reminding me of that." When her focus settled back on Walter, there was a knowing look in his eyes. She hadn't told him what had happened, but she didn't need to now. She'd said everything she needed to. "My anxiety...I can't explain what it does to me. I just know that I've done well for eight years now. I don't want to ruin my progress."

When Lou sat, Walter stood up slowly beside her. Surprised, Lou looked up and watched as he cleared his throat and looked around the room. His eyes landed on Lou again. "My name is Walter, but this little one over here likes to call me Walty. Don't call me Walty." The room laughed, including Walter, and he wiped the corners of his mouth before he continued. "I'm a recovering drug addict. Me and Lou met eight years ago at our first NA meeting." Walter rested a hand on her shoulder. "I served two tours in Iraq when I was a kid. Got blown up by an ATM-74 when I was out kicking sand. Nearly blew my damn leg off, but they fixed me up. Med Corps put me on oxy for the pain, and it helped for a while. Then I started gettin' addicted to the stuff, and it went downhill from there. Took me fifteen years, but I've been clean for a decade now." Scattered applause filled the room.

"Trouble is, my leg's been bothering me lately. I keep thinking I can get through it, but sometimes the urge is strong." Walter clicked his tongue. "My point is...if I can make it through the pain, so can you." While Walter was likely talking to everyone in the room, his eyes landed square on Lou's. She blinked through watery eyes, mouthing a 'thank you' under her breath. He smiled, taking his seat back beside her. A hand fell on her knee, squeezing it.

Sometimes, Lou wasn't sure what she'd do without him.

It was a quarter after eight when the meeting ended. After making small talk with some regulars and fetching a barely fresh muffin and decaf coffee, Lou joined Walter at their usual seats. "You feelin' better?" Walter asked sinking his teeth into a rather large blueberry muffin.

"Slow down there Walty, or you might choke," Lou warned him, letting out a laugh. She did feel better. It was amazing what talking about it did. "Yeah, I'm good. Thanks for coming." Walter looked up, and Lou continued on. "So your leg's been bothering you? Why didn't you tell me?" Her mind thought back to the other night at the bridge when he'd been limping and looked in pain. Lou should have asked then and was guilty now that she hadn't.

"Kid, if I was in trouble, I'd tell you." Walter said. "I'm just getting old."

Walter's explanation seemed reassuring, but something didn't sit well with Lou. Before she could think about it long, there was a nudge at her leg. Caspian whined, his big blue eyes staring up at her. "I guess that's my cue to leave," Lou decided, getting up from her seat. She downed the lukewarm coffee and held onto the muffin for the drive home. "You sure you don't want me to drive you home?"

"Kathy offered," Walter reminded her. "It's on her way, unlike it is for you."

Lou smiled at him. "I don't mind."

"Get outta here, kid." Walter waved her off, smiling back.

———

The 1920s Craftsman house sat at the end of a cul-de-sac on Portland's eastside. Painted a fresh slate gray color with cream white trim, it stood out on the street. Lou worked with her brother the previous summer to renovate the property that was in dire need of upkeep. Damask rose bushes lined the front porch, their leaves glowing in the yellow porch lights and the street lamp on the edge of the drive.

As soon as Caspian and Lou made it inside, the dog whined. He was likely antsy after spending the evening in a basement. Lou seemed to be on the same page as the dog. She sighed, looking at the clock. It was just after nine.

Typically, Lou didn't bring the dog home with her, but tonight had been an exception. It was late, and she hadn't felt like traveling back to Troutdale to drop him off at the training facility. So here he was.

Needy, as always.

"Fine, buddy." Lou stretched and looked around the room for his leash. "You win." Caspian barked a happy response as Lou snapped the buckle onto his collar and headed for the side door in the kitchen that led out to the driveway.

It was quiet out, as it often was at this time of night. An occasional car drove down the road as they made their way down the neighborhood sidewalk. Crickets chirped in the background as Caspian darted in and out of the grasses, sniffing out trees and bushes.

Lou turned on a familiar bigleaf maple lined street. The wind brought the smell of the trees to her, and she breathed it in along with the crisp evening air. It had been a long time since Lou had taken a detour in this part of the neighborhood. She usually did her best to avoid it, unless she was cutting through to go to work. Tonight, however, she was feeling reminiscent, and felt the desire to go back.

The houses on this street were newer than the ones on Lou's. They were all the same from when she was growing up as a kid. It was the street where Lou had first seen Alice Gray, who was Alice Ericson then, on the high school bus. They'd moved her senior year. She was waiting in the rain with a pastel pink and white umbrella and a matching slicker. Alice's blonde hair had been long then and was pulled up into a high ponytail. They'd both had the same Burton backpacks, gray and white. She'd sat in front of Lou, who always liked to ride near the back of the bus.

All the way to school, Lou watched her. She was reading a novel, but Lou couldn't remember what it was. Maybe Austen or Woolf. Alice always liked classic female authors. Lou couldn't stop looking at her, mesmerized by everything about her. She was the prettiest girl Lou had ever seen, by a longshot.

They sat together in AP Chemistry and Lou somehow brought up the book Alice had been reading, and although she knew nothing about it, she'd asked about it anyway. By the end of class, she knew more than she ever thought she would. Alice sat beside her on the bus ride home, and Lou learned all about her life in southern Portland before she'd moved. About her parents, James, the accountant, and Lily, the school teacher. Alice told her all about her plans to go to college to become a teacher and how her life had been figured out ever since she was a little girl.

Conversations with Alice were easy after that. It didn't take long after their first date at the roller-skating rink until they were sneaking kisses under the football bleachers and holding hands in empty hallways. Alice was natural. Effortless. Lou hadn't imagined life without her.

Until it had happened.

Lou paused in front of the familiar Craftsman house, a muted pastel yellow with white trim. The landscaping was immaculate, as it always was. While Lily was born with a green thumb, Alice couldn't keep a plant alive if she tried. Perhaps she'd gotten better over the years; Lou wouldn't have known.

The light in the dining room was on. Lou scanned the large sash windows in front of the house, surprised to see Lily and James sitting at the table. Across from them sat a familiar face. She couldn't make out Alice in great detail from the distance she was at, but she could tell it was her. They looked like they were eating, perhaps enjoying some late-night ice cream, which was a tradition with the Ericson's.

How long was it since Alice visited last? She must have been living in Seattle since they broke up. Was she still married to Jeremy? When Lou found out Alice had married her freshman boyfriend from high school, it had almost killed her. There were so many questions running through Lou's mind, she could hardly focus.

Caspian nudged against her, whining softly. Lou looked down at the dog, who seemed ready to go. When she glanced back up at the Ericson's house, the light in the dining room had flipped off. Sighing, Lou took off, back in the direction of her house, filled with anxiety over the idea that she and Alice would be near one another for four whole weeks. Lou wasn't sure if she could survive that long with Alice so close, not without asking questions she wasn't sure she wanted to know the answers to. Without admitting feelings that were still coursing inside of her.

Lou didn't have a choice. She had to make it, whether she liked it or not. And she decided, as she and the dog walked back together, that Caspian and Anna were the reason. She and Alice were a memory now, but the dog and his new owner...that was all that mattered.

At least that's what she was going to tell herself.

Chapter Six

The soft hum of classical music mingled with the rustling of leaves as a breeze blew by. Over the outside speakers, NPR played its two hours of Baroque music, which Lily often listened to while she worked in the yard. Alice watched her mother as she pruned abelia shrubs along the white picket fence. She relaxed back in the Amish rollback wooden swing that dangled from a perch under the trellis in the backyard. When she was younger, the old bench used to squeak when she'd rock back and forth, but since her father had bought a new one a few years back, it was as quiet as a mouse.

Alice got lost in thought for a while, admiring the beautiful morning. Inside, her father was feeding Anna bacon and eggs for breakfast. Instead of joining them, Alice had gone outside, anticipating a phone call.

When the phone buzzed in her hands, it caused Alice to jump slightly in surprise. She looked down, and sure enough Jeremy's name was stretched across the screen. Alice answered, putting the phone up to her ear after tucking hair behind it. "Jeremy?"

"Alice," Jeremy replied. By the sound of it, he was in the car.

"I'm on my way to work. What did you need so early? Is everything okay?"

For a moment, Alice felt rather silly for texting Jeremy in a panic when she'd woken up. She had no earthly idea why she'd done it, outside of being in a panic. It had been a year since their divorce. Alice had to stop depending on him so much. "I—" Alice tried to figure out exactly what she wanted to say. "Are you sure you can't come to Portland for a few weeks? Just for these classes? It would be really beneficial for you, too." It was the only excuse she could think of. The only thing she could figure that would possibly help her tamper the wave of emotions she'd been feeling since seeing Lou the previous day. "It's only for four weeks."

"A month is a long time, Al," Jeremy argued. "I've just started the new position. You know I would if I could. You can handle this. We'll figure it out when you get back." Alice sighed loudly into the phone before she could stop herself. "What's going on? Is Anna okay?"

"Anna's fine," Alice reassured him. She sunk back into the swinging bench, lifting her feet off the ground so it rocked a little. "I just…I was feeling a little overwhelmed is all."

"You sure?" Jeremy asked.

"Positive," Alice said, and then said her goodbyes quickly, before hanging up the phone. She hadn't given Jeremy a chance to press the issue further. Alice's heart was thudding in her chest, a little harder than normal. She fidgeted in her seat, as she noticed her mother coming up to meet her.

"Was that Jeremy?" Lily asked, sitting beside her on the bench. She removed a pair of cream white leather gardening gloves and sat them in her lap. Then she brushed a strand of her slightly graying blonde hair from her eyes and looked at Alice. She'd always admired how her mother had kept her hair natural instead of dyeing it. Lily had always been one to age gracefully, and Alice hoped that she too would be like that when she was her mother's age.

"Yes," Alice said, trying her best to maintain her composure. "I was just making sure he didn't want to come to Portland to do these classes with Anna and me."

Lily turned her head, swinging the bench lightly and wrapping her left hand around the metal chain that held it up on a wooden frame. "Alice, is everything alright?" Alice wondered why her mother asked the question until she elaborated. "We haven't talked about what happened in the car the other day..."

"Right now isn't the time…"

"Are you happy?" Lily asked, surprising her. Her mother's hazel eyes, that they shared, had softened with a look of genuine concern.

Alice sighed, reaching out to wrap her hands around her mother's. "Oh, Mom." She couldn't help but smile. "It was the right decision. I promise. Jeremy and I are both okay."

Though her look of unease hadn't completely faded, Lily's shoulders relaxed a bit and she leaned back into the swing. "Your father and I never meant to pressure you into anything, I hope you know that."

For a moment, Alice hesitated, surprised at what had come out of her mother's mouth. "What do you mean?"

"About getting married and having children. I hope you didn't do it just for our sakes," Lily said, her eyes filled with concern. "Your father and I just want to see you happy. That's all. And if Jeremy didn't make you happy, then we support you. No matter what." Alice watched as her mother reached out her hand to squeeze her own. Alice sighed.

"I know that, Mom," Alice gave her a small smile. "I wanted kids and a family too. And I thought Jeremy was the answer to all of that. He's a wonderful man. I'm sure he's going to make someone very happy. But we weren't meant to be. And that's okay. I'm okay."

"Well something is the matter," Lily argued, staring Alice down. "You're not yourself."

The thought came briefly, that Alice could lie about what was really going on in her mind in that moment. She could ignore the fact that inside she was in a great deal of turmoil. Instead, something compelled her to tell Lily exactly what was on her mind. "I ran into Lou yesterday."

It only took Lily a half second before her eyes grew wide. "Louise Pearson?"

"Mom, you know she doesn't like to be called Louise," Alice scolded her, and then quickly was in disbelief that she had. What did it matter to her what her mother called her? She and Lou hadn't seen or spoken to one another in nearly a decade. "And yes, that Lou. She's a trainer at the Guide Dog Association."

Lily looked lost in thought for a moment. "Did she say anything to you?"

"We barely said anything to one another," Alice admitted. "What am I supposed to say to her? It's been eight years." Eight years, yet somehow the feelings were still so intense, it seemed like it was only yesterday they'd last seen one another. And Alice had no idea why. "I don't know if I can be in the same room with her for a month. That's why I called Jeremy."

Alice expected that maybe her mother would suggest that she or her father might be able to come in Jeremy's place. Surprisingly though, it was not what came out of her mouth. "Maybe you should talk with her." The bench stopped rocking and her mother turned her full attention to Alice.

"I'm not going to *talk* with her," Alice argued, realizing that her voice had grown a half-octave louder and more defensive. "I don't have anything to say to her."

"You certainly seem like you have something to say to her," Lily retorted.

Alice shoved an angry reply down, realizing she'd gotten far more worked up about the situation than she'd meant to. Perhaps her mother wasn't wrong. All these feelings that were bubbling to the surface needed to be dealt with. Except, Alice didn't want to deal with them. She wanted to get Caspian and get out of town. As far away from her past as she could get.

"I just have to get through the next few weeks," Alice decided firmly.

———

The dog's eyes were as blue as a perfect spring sky, his expression warmer than the gentle sunlight that peeked through the chiffon trimmed windows of the Portland Guide Dog Association training center. Caspian stared at Anna's small hand that was suspended in front of her.

Tammy squatted down beside her. "Okay, Anna," she said, touching her arm gently and helping her extend her hand and palm outward "Hold your hand out like I'm showing you. You want to tell Caspian 'touch' and wait for him to touch your hand. As soon as he does, give him a treat. Okay?" Anna nodded. "Whenever you're ready, sweetheart."

"Touch, Caspian!" Anna said firmly. The dog studied her for a half second, before his white paw swung into the air and tapped her hand. A gentle laugh escaped Anna. "Good doggie," she said, handing him a handful of treats.

Alice looked up across the room, searching. When she found the familiar bright red hair, she paused. Today, Lou had it pinned up behind her in a messy bun. The sight of it brought back memories of washing dishes in their old college apartment. Placing kisses in the crook of her neck as she scrubbed plates in the sink. Lou's hair had always smelled like strolling through an herb garden, with hints of lavender, thyme, sage and rosemary. If Alice thought on it long enough, she still remembered the scent faintly. She sucked in a long breath of air, letting it roll out of her nostrils.

"I'm going to go get some more treats," Tammy's soft voice interrupted Alice's daydreaming and brought her back to the room. Caspian was enjoying a head scratch from Anna, while Tammy disappeared to the other side of the room. Alice watched her daughter with the dog, admiring how gentle he was with her.

Lou's laughter erupted from across the room. Laughter that had always held Alice captive, every time she heard it. There was a huge smile stretched across Lou's face while she was kneeling to offer the dog she was working with affection. Alice watched her transfixed, up until she noticed Lou had turned slightly and was staring right at her. It was impossible to breathe then. Alice shifted her gaze back to her daughter and to Tammy.

"Let's try to get him to sit," Tammy said, kneeling down beside Anna. "You'll want to reach out and touch him so you know he's sitting. Okay?" Tammy took Alice's daughter's small hand and let it fall on Caspian's backside. "Now, ask him to sit, Anna."

"Sit, Caspian," Anna said, confidently, using the command that Tammy had taught her. She leaned against her mother for support, while she faced forward toward the dog. Alice imagined that she'd made out his blurry shape in front of her. The dog immediately sat and Anna reached out to feel that he'd done what she'd asked, before handing him a treat. "Good doggie."

Alice looked up at Tammy, who was smiling broadly. "Good job, Anna. Now tell him to lay and use this hand signal. You want to make your hand go to the ground, like this." Tammy took Anna's small hand in her own and demonstrated the motion, before letting her try it on her own.

Anna's focus honed in on the dog, and she lowered her palm flat, facing the ground. "Lay, Caspian." Again, the dog immediately did what she asked. Anna reached forward and felt to make sure the dog had done what she'd asked of him. He was impressively obedient. Something that the training facility must have owed to Lou, since she was the one to train him.

Thinking about her caused Alice's attention to drift once more. Alice's eyes scanned across the room, finding Lou almost immediately in the crowd. It was hard not to watch her, wrapped up in her element as she helped another family with their dog. She was so patient, so calm. Content. Alice wondered how much she'd changed over the past eight years.

It definitely seemed like she was happy. Like she was significantly more put together than she had been the last time they'd been together. The idea that Lou was better made Alice feel a mix of emotions. Happy for her that she'd figured out her life, but a strange mix of sadness too, that she couldn't quite explain.

Good for her, Alice thought, finally shaking the thoughts of Lou from her brain.

"Let's try one more time and then we'll be done for the day," Tammy suggested, looking down at Anna. Alice's attention focused back on her daughter and the dog, while they worked through a series of commands a final time. When they'd finished, Anna said goodbye to Caspian and Alice took her hand carefully. The two made their way across the room, and Alice gathered her belongings from one of the benches. When they'd nearly gotten to the door, she was conscious that Lou was standing alone with the black Labrador she'd been working with all morning—hovering by the door as if she wanted them to meet.

They studied each other for a half-second. Finally, Alice couldn't stand it anymore. "Lou—"

The expression on Lou's face read so many things at once. Mostly though, it looked pained. Anxious. She shook her head quickly and turned her attention between the dog she was holding onto and Alice's daughter. "Have a good night you two," Lou said quickly, tugging at the dog's leash. The dog sat up quickly and followed at Lou's side. Lou didn't spend another second dwelling on either of them. Instead, Alice watched as she darted quickly across the room, disappearing faster than she could ever have imagined possible… realizing that her chance of talking with her ex might be more difficult than she'd ever anticipated.

And maybe even still, after all this time, some things hadn't changed after all.

Chapter Seven

The blue and red lights were little more than smudgy illuminations in the slanting rain, but beneath their glow was the white bodywork of a police car. Its yellow-white headlights shone on the dense hedgerow where Lou was standing with a black umbrella and teal blue rain slicker. Detective Kennedy looked like a knight in his white Charger, black tires squealing on the blacktop as he slid to a halt in the downpour.

Lou ran to the passenger-side door, just as he unlocked it. She fell into the dark gray leather seating, buckling herself in shortly after. "Where are we headed tonight?"

Scratchy static filled the car, followed by a slew of words that Lou could barely catch from a female police officer, or a dispatcher, she wasn't sure which. Rick picked up the microphone, putting it close to his shaggy mustache, before speaking clearly. "Headed that direction. Just picked up the rookie."

"Rookie?" Lou raised a brow as the detective snapped the mic back in place on the dash.

"Lady just got evicted from a house outside of Hillsboro. Hoarder. Guess she liked hoarding animals, too. Where's your girlfriend?" Lou frowned at him, knowing full well he was playing with her. "I mean Meg. Pardon me."

"Should be a few minutes behind us, last time I talked to her. She talked with Peggy at the station and got the address." Lou turned her attention outside to the gloomy evening and the rain-drops pattering around them as they drove down the barren street. Lou kept mostly to herself.

"Thinking hard?" Kennedy asked, turning down the static on the radio a bit. Lou could feel his eyes glancing at her.

"No, why?" Lou turned her attention back to Detective Kennedy, who was smirking underneath his bushy graying brown facial fur.

"You're quieter than I've ever known you," he replied. The car made a sharp right turn and Lou grabbed a hold of the door frame to keep herself steady. "Roads are slick tonight." Lou didn't argue with him about her ominous mood, or about the condition of the roads. Instead, she sat quietly as they made the rest of their drive.

When they finally pulled into a driveway leading up to the hoarder's house, Lou felt a lurch in her stomach. It wasn't nervous-ness, like she often felt on other ride-alongs with Kennedy over the years. Instead, it was almost anticipation in a way. Something to keep her mind busy. Off of other things that she wanted desperately to stop thinking about.

Megan had already arrived with the Humane Society van, waiting in the driveway. There was no one else waiting, Kennedy being the only police officer called to the scene. It wasn't mandatory for him to be there, but it was dark, and the woman had just been evicted. Better safe than sorry, Lou supposed.

She watched as Kennedy hopped out of the car and followed shortly behind. The door snapped shut behind her. Megan approached them, carrying a catchpole and a backpack full of supplies. "Peggy told me this lady had something like thirty cats and there are also some dogs. I don't know if we'll have room for all of them." She handed Lou and Detective Kennedy each a surgical mask, before strapping one to her face. "You're going to need it. Trust me."

"We'll try," Lou said, trudging after Kennedy in the rain, taking shelter under Megan's paisley umbrella. Her wavy red hair whipped in the wind as they made their way up the stairs of the rather elaborate looking American Colonial mansion. It stretched farther back than Lou could even see through the rain. She could only imagine what was waiting for them inside the house.

While Lou had been looking forward to witnessing another one of Detective Kennedy's marvelous kick-downs of the doorway, she was relieved to see he was armed with a key that evening. He unlocked the deadbolt of the dark brown stained door and pushed it open. Lou watched him struggle, pushing gruffly against it until it partially opened.

"I'm warning you ladies, I've been told it's pretty rough in here." Kennedy disappeared beyond the door, flipping on a switch by the wall. The room illuminated, just as Lou followed in behind him. Dusty yellow light scattered across a sea of books, newspapers and magazines piled nearly as high as Lou. There was a small path to the right of the door, which Kennedy took. They went in single file, straight through what Lou could only imagine was at one time a living room. Now it looked like a storage facility and even through the mask, she could smell the pungent stench of ammonia.

"Lou," Megan called out to her from behind, and she took pause. A gray tabby was walking over stacks of paper. It looked thin and malnourished. Lou watched as Megan held out a treat to the animal and it darted over at rapid speed. As soon as it was in reach, she scooped it up and into a crate. "I'll take this one outside. Be back in a minute." Before she left, she handed Lou the catchpole, and Lou took it carefully.

Megan turned as best she could through the debris and made her way back out of the house. Meanwhile, Rick and Lou ventured onward. Lou couldn't remember smelling something so bad. She pulled her shirt up around her mouth and nose, doing her best not to breathe it in. It smelled like a mixture of mildew and rot. Where it was coming from, Lou had no idea. Detective Kennedy took a right into another room and Lou followed behind.

While there were no papers in the dining room, there were

enough knick-knacks to last a lifetime. Lou had never seen piles of stuff so high in her life. Just like the main room, there was barely any room to walk. "I think there's a few pups up here," Kennedy said, nodding toward the kitchen. Sure enough, they made it inside and found several crates with puppies sitting on the floor. An adult dog was lying beside it, sleeping soundly. He was thin, some sort of scruffy Pointer mix with gray and white fur.

Lou cautiously approached, squatting down beside him. The dog lifted his head, eyeing her carefully. He didn't look dangerous in the least. Mellow, if anything. Lou sat the catchpole against the counter, which was littered with pots and pans of every variety. She put a hand forward, cautiously letting the dog sniff it. The Pointer mix leaned forward, smelling her hand for a few seconds. Soon after, he leaned into it, nudging his head against her palm.

"Well look at that. Lou made a friend." When Lou turned her attention to Kennedy, he had a stupid grin on his face. Lou gave him a look before she focused back on the dog.

"It's okay, buddy," Lou said quietly, stretching her hand around his head to give him a scratch behind the ears. "We are going to get all of you guys out of here now." She sat up, looking at Kennedy. "You think you can help me with some of these puppies?"

Detective Kennedy was probably one of the few police officers that Lou had met over the years that had an affinity for animals. She was surprised he'd never requested to keep a rescue for himself. Instead of replying, he squatted down, opening up the cage, studying the dogs. Carefully, he lifted two of the four puppies from the cage, cradling them against his chest. Lou shut the crate behind them. She studied the scruffy dog sitting by the cages and wondered for a minute what she was going to do with him.

Finally, she lifted the dog from the floor into her arms. He wasn't too heavy, quite underweight for his height. The dog didn't seem to mind the lift, leaning against her sleepily. "I wonder if she wanted to take any of these animals," Lou said thoughtfully.

"Technically, all these animals are the new owner's property," Kennedy explained as they weaved their way back out of the house. "They asked for them all to be removed along with all of the woman's belongings. The folks were even nice enough to sell her stuff to give her some money to live on."

Lou pondered on what he'd said for a moment. "It's a shame though, isn't it? If she wanted some of these animals, just to lose them all in an instant seems pretty devastating." It wasn't the same exact situation, but a little part of Lou felt that way with Caspian. Though it felt different now knowing he was going to Alice and her daughter. Something about it brought her a little more comfort, since Lou knew he'd be well taken care of.

They made it the rest of the way outside, meeting Megan in the driveway. She approached Lou first, offering to take the dog. "I've got him," Lou reassured her. Megan approached Kennedy, who dropped the two pups in her arms.

"I'll go get the other two," he said, taking off back toward the house. Meanwhile, Lou followed Megan back to the Humane Society van. As soon as she brought the dog down to the crate, he started to whimper, pawing at her backside.

"Looks like he's attached to you," Megan said, trying to offer a hand. The dog was stubborn, holding tightly to Lou.

"Let me have a minute," Lou said, looking at Megan. "Go back inside and help Kennedy. I'll be back in a few."

Megan nodded and took off again, while Lou sat down on the floor of the open van, cradling the dog. "You're really freaked out, aren't you, bud?" The dog leaned against her and Lou could feel him shivering in her arms. "I've got you. You're going to be just fine." Lou's fingers brushed down the back of the dog's fur in long, solid strokes, trying her best to be as comforting as she could be.

When the dog finally relaxed, Lou dropped him down into an open cage in the van, and he went in sleepily. She locked the door behind him and stayed sitting, watching him through the metal bars. Lou admired his shaggy looks and his graying fur. The dog reminded her a lot of her childhood pet, Benji. They somehow shared a likeness that she couldn't explain.

"How about I call you Benji?" Lou said, thoughtfully. She stuck her fingers through the bars of the cage, letting the dog sniff and run his muzzle alongside them. "That sound good to you?" The dog seemed content, curling up in a ball and laying on the floor, closing his eyes. Lou decided it must have been, since he had no complaints, and smiled softly to herself at the thought. "Okay, Benji it is."

———

L ou stood in the doorway, looking out into the gravel yard where Caspian and the other Labrador Retrievers were stretching their legs and running around in the unusually sunny Portland morning. There was still an hour before classes began, and despite her cheerful surroundings, there was a horrible sinking feeling in Lou's chest about seeing Alice again today.

She'd been lost in thought and hadn't seen Tammy appear beside her. "Where are you at?"

The dogs were barking in the distance. Something had caught their attention outside of the fence. Probably a bird or a squirrel, Lou guessed. She turned to Tammy, shrugging. "Nothing. Just distracted a little, I guess."

"About Alice?" Tammy guessed. While Lou loved Tammy dearly, sometimes she hated the fact that someone knew so much about her that they could read her like an open book. The only other person that knew that much personal information was Walter, and even he freaked her out sometimes. Maybe it was her anxiety getting the best of her again.

"Yeah," Lou finally admitted, turning her attention back to Tammy. Those intelligent brown eyes were studying her intensely, with a look of concern stretched across her face.

"Avoiding her isn't going to solve the problem," Tammy stated.

"I know," Lou replied, watching Caspian dart across the yard, kicking up rocks as he went. Phil, one of the other Labradors, chased after him. They looked so happy. So carefree. Lou had never wished that she could be a dog more in her life than in that moment.

She needed a reason to get far, far away from here.

"I want you to work with her today," Tammy decided, and her words made Lou's blood run cold. She opened her mouth to argue, but Tammy stopped her almost immediately. "I know you're going to tell me no, but you can't run from your problems, Lou. Isn't that what got you in trouble in the first place? You can do this."

"I don't think I can," Lou said, feeling her pulse elevate in her neck, to the point that it was throbbing almost painfully.

"You've got to be brave," Tammy argued with her, reaching out to place a hand on her shoulder. The reassuring touch instantly calmed Lou a little, despite the fact that her nerves were still getting the best of her. "It's only for a few weeks. And who knows, it might be good for you two to talk to each other?"

The last thing on earth Lou wanted to do was talk to Alice Gray. Especially after the way things had ended. What would she even say? There weren't enough words to convey how sorry she'd been. How much she'd spent the last eight years of her life trying to make amends for that terrible part of her life. And for what? Tammy was right, she was falling back into the same hole that had gotten her into trouble in the first place. Her anxiety was getting the better of her, yet again.

Lou took a deep breath and closed her eyes for a second. "Okay. I'll do it."

The little ounce of confidence that Tammy had instilled in Lou immediately vanished later that morning when the parents started to arrive. Not unlike the first day of training, Alice had gotten there first with Anna. When she entered, Lou had remained frozen, until Alice had scanned the room and found her standing with Caspian. Lou sucked in a rather deep breath of air and slowly trudged forward to meet her.

Caspian immediately went to greet Anna, who squealed happily when he did. "Hi, Caspian!" Anna said, running her fingers over his face and head. "Good doggie."

Meanwhile, Alice's attention was still on Lou, whose anxiety was threatening to murder her. Her heart was thudding so hard in her chest and her palms were so sweaty, she thought she'd pass out at any moment.

Breathe, she begged herself. Lou's eyes were unable to meet

Alice's directly. Instead, she decided to focus on Anna. "Hi Anna. It's Lou. Remember me from the first class?"

"Hi Lou!" Anna replied, her head turning in the direction of Lou's voice. "You were the one who told me Caspian was twenty years old in human years." Lou laughed, surprised she'd remembered such a small detail.

"That's right. How do you feel about me helping you today?"

"Instead of Tammy?" Anna asked, still running her hands over Caspian's face, who seemed rather content with the affection.

"Instead of Tammy," Lou agreed. "Is that okay?"

"Sure," Anna said, smiling. "Is that okay Mama?"

Finally, somehow, Lou managed to look at Alice. Just for a moment. Alice was staring at her. Hard. "That's fine," Alice replied, but her eyes conveyed otherwise. Like she was completely unsure of what was happening. Nearly as much as Lou was. And as much as Lou was convinced she wasn't going to make it through this alive, now she had no choice. She'd committed and would have to follow through.

"Okay," Lou said, her eyes turning back to Anna and Caspian. "We're going to have Caspian come to you when he's called. How does that sound?" Anna nodded. "Okay, I'm going to walk away a few paces and I'll tell you when to call for him. You're going to say 'Caspian, come,' got it?" The little girl nodded again and Lou turned on a heel, leading Caspian beside her as they trailed a short distance across the room.

Don't look at her. Don't look at her. Lou begged herself once she'd spun back around to face Anna and Alice. Clearly Lou lacked any self-restraint whatsoever because her eyes immediately fell on Alice's hazel ones, that were staring right back at her. There was an unreadable expression stretched across her face, which made Lou that much more anxious. She brought her mind back to the dog and Anna, trying to stay focused. "Okay, Anna. Call him to you whenever you're ready." Lou unlatched Caspian's leash from his halter.

The dog waited for a few seconds until Anna's small but confident voice rang out across the room. "Come, Caspian!" Caspian didn't hesitate, walking straight forward in the direction of Anna.

Even with all of the commotion around the room, even with other commands from parents and kids and trainers alike, the dog's focus was completely on Anna. The minute he reached the little girl, he nudged into her stomach with his face.

Anna giggled and her hands found his face again. Lou immediately followed after the dog, and once she'd reached Anna, she gently took her hand. She put a handful of treats in her palm, which Caspian immediately took, graciously. "We're going to give him some treats every time he does what we say," Lou explained. Once Caspian had broken away a little, Lou planted more treats in Anna's hands. "Put those in your pocket for now. We'll use them again in a minute. For now, we're going to have Caspian lead you straight to your mom. You ready to try it?"

Generally, they didn't start working on this sort of thing until the second week of classes, but Caspian and Anna seemed to be bonding so well, Lou wanted to try anyway. Alice was squatting down near the floor next to Anna, "Do you mind if we try it?" Lou directed her question to Alice. Lou could tell that Alice was nervous. While Lou had never had a child, she'd worked with enough anxious parents to know that look when she saw it.

"Okay, just stand here with Caspian until I say go, Anna. Then you're going to tell him to 'lead me to mama,' nice and loud, okay?" Lou waited for Anna to nod that she understood and then gave her a soft squeeze on the shoulder. "Okay, I'm going to go on the other side with your mom. Just wait for a minute and we'll try it."

Anna nodded again and Lou gestured to Alice indicating that she should follow her. While they were only a few yards away from Anna, Lou was feeling a little nervous herself. Whether it was from trying something hard so early, or the fact that she was now only a few feet away from the former love of her life, or both… she couldn't tell. Maybe she didn't want to know.

"Are you sure she's going to be okay? Maybe I should help her this time around…" Alice turned to look at Lou, who smiled at her softly.

"She'll be fine. We have to start somewhere, right? If anything goes wrong, I'll get to her. I promise." Lou felt a weird urge to reach out and give Alice a reassuring touch. It was something she hadn't expected of herself. Especially given the circumstances. But there it was, a random fleeting feeling that she needed to comfort Alice. Like no time had passed between them and that their painful breakup had never happened. But she stopped herself. Lou shook the thoughts from her head and turned her attention to Anna.

"Let's give it a try. Tell Caspian what to do when you're ready."

There was a long pause after Lou spoke, where nothing happened. The dog waited patiently beside her until Anna finally spoke. "Lead me to mama, Caspian!" Anna gripped the top of the halter, where the handle was, and the dog took off slowly. Meanwhile, Lou motioned him to keep steady and slow, and pointed at Alice to help guide him, hoping that her hand gestures were enough.

Caspian seemed to respond well, taking his time as he moved forward. Lou held her breath, watching as Anna took wobbly steps toward them. "Almost there," Alice finally said, as her daughter drew closer. The minute she was within arm's reach, Alice took her and squeezed her tightly. "You did it!" As soon as he'd reached them, Caspian sat. Lou handed him treats and then scratched him on top of his head.

"Tell Caspian, 'good job,'" Lou reminded Anna.

"Good job, Caspian!" Anna said, turning to try and find him. Alice guided Anna's hand forward, so that she could touch the dog. The child's hands wrapped around Caspian's face and she pressed them together. Caspian licked Anna's cheek gently, but Lou decided not to scold him for it. Lou breathed a long sigh of relief, a joyful warmth spreading through her. The dog had done his job. Years of training was paying off.

Alice and Lou exchanged glances, and before Lou could stop her, Alice had wrapped her arms around her neck. "Thank you," she said, nearly breathlessly and full of emotion. Her voice cracked slightly as she conveyed the heartfelt words. Lou froze in place, every fiber of her body exploding with panic. She didn't know what to do, what to think. A whirlwind of emotions rippled through her, caught in Alice's grasp. There was a familiar smell of honey and wildflowers. The same shampoo she'd used ever since they'd been dating. There was the firmness of her grip. Light and tender, yet sturdy and safe. Like it had been all those years ago. The proximity they were in was so overwhelming that Lou barely managed to suck air into her chest.

Was she ever going to escape this woman?

It seemed as if Alice was just as paralyzed. Like they were both trapped in some timeless void, where everything stood still for longer than just a few short moments. Then suddenly, like a bolt of lightning had unexpectedly struck her, those feelings came back. Feelings that were still raging through her like they'd only broken up yesterday. Only Alice wasn't *her* Alice anymore. Not the Alice she'd once loved. Lou was the woman who had destroyed their life together. And Alice would never be the same person again. Not in Lou's eyes.

Lou cleared her throat, unable to look directly at Alice. "So, typically we let the dogs go home or to the hotel with their new owners every weekend. I've talked it over with Tammy, and she thinks it would be a good idea for Caspian to go with you and Anna for the next few days so he can start getting acclimated to being around you. What do you say?"

Anna heard the conversation and squeaked loudly. "Can we please, Mama? Please?"

It looked as though Alice was thinking hard for a few seconds, before she relaxed and smiled. "I think that would be a good idea. You aren't going to miss him too much?" Alice asked.

Lou broke into a small smile. Just a hint. "I'll be crying myself to sleep tonight."

Truthfully, Lou was already missing the dog and he hadn't even left yet. But she knew that the time was coming soon enough. And if there was any person in the whole world that Lou knew would take care of Caspian as well as she had these past few years, it was Alice Gray and her daughter.

Chapter Eight

"Oh look how pretty he is," Lily mused, as Alice, Anna and Caspian made their way through the side door into the remodeled galley kitchen. Lavish Honduran mahogany cabinets complimented the pristinely clean aspen white granite countertops. Every detail of this kitchen had been designed from top to bottom with care and precision. Cooking, like gardening, was Lily's pride and joy.

In this moment Alice knew how much Lily loved her grand-daughter. Not once did she comment about the fine dog hairs that would undoubtedly cling to her throw pillows or complain about the dirty paw prints that would likely muddy her pristine floors.

Instead, Lily was ecstatic, to say the least.

"I'll keep him in the guest suite downstairs with us," Alice reassured her, even though it was likely Lily wouldn't have made a fuss even if the dog ran lose around the house. Caspian looked up at Alice's mother with his beautiful blue eyes. Lily gave him a long once-over, as a smile broke across her face. . "Thank you," she mouthed to Alice, who nodded and smiled back at her mother. "I have a chicken in the oven that needs to be taken out. Dinner will be ready in a few minutes." Before Alice could thank her or get another word in edgewise, her mother disappeared across the room, fetching the food.

"I'm not particularly hungry," Alice mentioned to her father quietly. In fact, she was so lost in thought and distracted, that all she wanted was to have a few moments of peace and quiet. "Can you save me some food for later? I'm going to let Caspian outside."

James gave an affirmative nod, placing a hand on Anna's shoulder. "Let's go wash our hands for dinner."

Alice wove her way through the hallway to the back door, leading outside. Caspian followed at her heel without being asked, though she kept a hold of his leash anyway. Once they'd made it outside, she released him and let him go explore. While he did, Alice sat on the swinging bench, laying back against the wood. She stared up through the slats in the trellis above, admiring the peach colored sky that was mingling with the blue as the sun started to set for the day.

When Alice closed her eyes, she thought of Lou, staring at her with those penetrating blue eyes. Her untamed garnet red hair drawn across her shoulder. The way her lips pursed when she was deep in thought. How she'd felt so comfortable in her embrace again, like it was natural and effortless and meant to be.

Too comfortable.

Alice had been lost in thought for a while, gently swaying on the bench. When she finally came to, it was because the screen door had snapped suddenly. When she turned her head to look in the direction of the sound, her father was standing a few feet away. "You might like to try some of your mother's chicken," he noted. "It was delicious." His gaze was fixed on Caspian, who was busy sniffing and rustling through Lily's rose bushes that lined the fences. "I'm sure your mother would love to know that dog was peeing in her damasks." James was grinning as he said it and Alice couldn't help but laugh.

"I won't tell her if you don't," she replied, as her father came to join her on the bench.

"I always liked this view" James looked out across the yard, and Alice followed. She sucked in a deep breath of air, fresh and crisp.

Alice had visited a number of cities in her life, but nothing quite compared to the air in Portland. Something about it was magical.

"Mom knows what she's doing," Alice agreed. They sat in silence after that, taking in the evening air and rocking softly. Alice leaned into her father's shoulder, letting her head fall down against it. His cheek laid against the top of her head, and Alice sighed. It had felt like forever since they'd sat like this. Maybe since college, Alice couldn't even remember now.

"Your mother told me about Lou," James said quietly, as if he had read Alice's mind. Alice felt her body stiffen, and then slowly she rose back up to a sitting position. Her body turned slightly to focus on him. Her father's back straightened, and he raised a brow. "That serious, huh?"

"She's the one that trained Caspian," Alice explained, glancing at the dog. He was busy inspecting an oak tree, why Lou had no idea. "We've been working together. I'm not sure I'm handling it very well."

James looked at a loss for words. Alice felt his hand fall onto her back, running his fingers across in slow, delicate motions. The way he used to comfort her when she was younger. She sighed, leaning back into his touch. Finally, he spoke. "Have you talked with her?"

"I've mostly been trying to avoid her," Alice admitted. "I don't know what to say. It's been eight years." She bit her lip lightly. "I didn't realize I still had all these unresolved emotions after all this time."

All these emotions had to be the understatement of the year. It was all she could think about, even when she was trying to think about the dog. Even when she was trying to think about her daughter. Lou was mixed somewhere in the middle, tangled up in everything about her life right then. As much as Alice had tried to forget her, to make any excuse for her not to be a part of her every waking moment, there she was. Beautiful, calm, serene Lou, with her knock-em-dead smile.

It made her insides hurt.

James shrugged. "You two need to talk." His voice had grown slightly sterner. "There's a lot of history there. You never ended it properly. No wonder you feel the way you do. I think anyone would be feeling that way in your position."

"What am I supposed to do?"

"Talk to her," James urged, nudging her gently. Alice sighed, unsure if that was the answer she wanted. Perhaps it was what she needed to hear. "Talk to her and work it out."

"What if she doesn't want to talk?" Alice asked, thinking about when she'd been shut down before. It was hard enough to be around her, nevertheless bring up memories that had been buried deep for years now.

"You'll never know unless you try," James replied. "Besides, I think it would do you both good. Especially since you're going to be around her for…what?"

"Three more weeks." Alice grimaced. "I don't know how I'm going to stand being in her presence that long."

"Talk to her," James repeated, squeezing her shoulder. "I promise it will help."

A nna was snuggled under the plush cotton sheets of the guest bed. Once Alice had finished tucking her in for the evening, she sat on the edge, looking down at Caspian. He was curled up at the foot of the bed, head resting on Anna's feet. He focused on her with his big blue eyes, staring deeply. Alice wondered what was going on in his mind, if he was missing Lou, or if he was content with them. Either way, it looked as though he'd found a spot to rest.

Once she felt satisfied, Alice left her daughter and returned to the living room adjacent to the bedroom. It was dark and quiet. A brown leather sofa sat on the far side of the room, facing a television. Alice sunk into the couch, switching on the lamp on the end table beside her. She fetched a book from her purse, a John Grisham novel she'd been meaning to finish.

Her mind was racing a thousand miles an hour. Even after her conversation earlier with her father and the rest of the evening to relax, she still felt agitated and like her brain couldn't settle. The reading didn't seem to be helping either.

Just as she'd gotten into a rhythm with her book, she felt a nudge at her feet. When Alice looked down, Caspian was staring up at her. He let out a quiet whine and pawed at her knee softly. "Feeling antsy too?" Alice asked. Judging by the expression on his face, it seemed she was correct.

Alice got up from her seat, making her way upstairs quietly with the dog and decided that she would take Caspian for a short walk. Thunder rumbled just as Alice gave a quick look outside. It was barely drizzling. Even with the storm approaching, she figured she could make it at least once around the block. She grabbed her raincoat off the hook by the front door and stuffed her feet into some sneakers.

A noise from the hall turned her attention elsewhere. James was standing outside of her parents' bedroom, wrapped in a red plaid robe, salt and pepper hair in disarray. "What are you doing up? And where are you going?"

The small yawn that escaped Alice seemed to indicate that she didn't know the answer to either question. She was certainly tired, but still antsy nonetheless. "I was going to take Caspian on a quick walk. We're both feeling a little restless."

James shot a glance outside. "It looks like it's about to storm."

"We'll be quick," Alice promised, as she opened the front door leading out onto the porch. "Don't worry." James had made his way to the doorway, and Alice turned around to lean in and plant a soft kiss on his cheek.

"Be quick," James repeated, nodding at the sky. Alice took off after that, without another word. The dog stuck by her side, well trained and obedient as ever. The pair made their way down the driveway and on to the sidewalk. Outside of the drizzle and the distant lightning and thunder, it was a calm night out. Alice had always enjoyed the pattering sound of rain as it fell. You almost had to enjoy rain if you lived in this area, since it was more often wet than not.

Alice looked down at the dog, who almost seemed to know she

was looking at him and looked back at her. Those blue eyes were as captivating as ever, and in that moment, Caspian reminded her of Lou. Alice was still in disbelief that they'd reconnected. And not only that, but that they were working together side-by-side again.

She had seemed more put together than the last time they'd been together. It was clear she enjoyed her work. Alice was worried after she quit graduate school that Lou would never find a job that would be as rewarding as wanting to be a veterinarian. It had been something she'd wanted to do since she was young. It seemed, however, that she had now found her calling. And that training guide dogs had been a perfect job for her temperament. Alice wondered too, if Lou had found someone to love. If she was happier since the last time that they had been together. The idea was bittersweet, on one hand she was glad that Lou had found peace, but on the other, she felt saddened that it hadn't been with her.

Caspian turned a corner and Alice drifted onto another street. It wasn't until she concentrated on her surroundings that she realized they were on Lou's family's home street. The house they'd spent so much time growing up in. How she had ended up there, she had no idea. It must have been a subconscious decision, her mind playing tricks on her.

Alice scanned down the street a few houses, realizing they were nearing the house. She wondered if Lou's father was still alive. The last time she'd been around him, he had been very sick. Alice remembered how sad she'd been for Lou, she had lost her mother at such a young age and it was likely she'd be losing her father too. Stephen was still around at least. Hopefully, anyway.

There was a tug on the leash. Alice's attention focused on Caspian. Before she could stop it, the dog had slipped out from under her and took off down the sidewalk in a mad dash. Alice watched him scamper across the front yard of one of the nearby houses. He was headed straight down toward Lou's childhood home.

She couldn't believe her luck. Was this really happening? Was she really about to lose the dog her first night having him? And not just any dog, but a dog that had been trained by Lou? Alice sucked in a deep breath of air and took off as fast as her feet could carry her. "Caspian!" The dog didn't even look back, disappearing behind the side of the house that had belonged to Lou's family.

Alice, who was more out of shape than she realized, was panting lightly as she turned the corner around the side of the house. Caspian was standing on the side porch of the Craftsman, stopped in front of a body that was slouched on the ground. "What are you doing here, buddy?"

That voice. It took moment to realize whose it was. It sounded weak and trembling, and as Alice veered closer, she realized Lou's body was shaking as her hand rested on top of Caspian's head. "Lou?"

Chapter Nine

The late evening sky was filled with tumultuous, dark, ragged clouds. The wind was sighing and thrashing in the treetops, and the boughs moaned. Lou sat up, just as a flash of forked lightning sprawled across the sky, illuminating everything around it. A peal of thunder followed shortly after, jerking her from bed.

She stared into the darkness, glazed eyes reading the clock on her nightstand. It was late. Or early. Either way, Lou wished she was still asleep. Instead, a wave of panic had overtaken her. Even though she'd woken unexpectedly, part of her was grateful. Her dreams had been filled with old memories of days when her life had been simple and complete. Old memories of a love she was longing for once again and shouldn't be. She couldn't get Alice Gray out of her mind, no matter how hard she was trying to.

Frustrated, Lou decided to get up from bed. She stumbled sleepily down the hall and toward the kitchen, thinking that perhaps a cup of tea might relax her enough for sleep. She rustled through the cupboard for the tin box full of tea bags and set it on the counter top. Afterward, she put on the kettle and sat down across the room at the wooden kitchen table.

Lightning flashed outside, and the rain tapped a gentle beat against the windows and on the roof. Lou listened quietly, admiring the sound. She'd always loved the rain, ever since she was a little kid. She stared out into the kitchen, admiring its small simplicity. This was the house she grew up in as a kid, the one she'd lived in all through high school and college. The house that had only been a few streets from Alice, yet they'd never known one another until high school. The house so near to where Alice was sleeping. Where Caspian was sleeping, while Lou was here alone.

It felt quiet. Too quiet.

The kettle interrupted her thoughts, shrieking into the room. Lou jumped up from her chair, racing across the room to pull it from the burner. As soon as she did, she rooted through the tin can for a bag of chamomile tea. Lou poured hot water into the cup and then resumed her spot at the kitchen table.

There was a noise outside that Lou first mistook as the wind. She looked briefly out the window over the table and saw nothing, so she ignored it. The noise rustled again a few seconds later, and this time Lou was certain it was something. There was a cold chill that was ripping down her spine, and her heart was speeding up in her chest. There was something or someone outside.

Lou got to her feet, making her way over to the side door that led out to the driveway. She cracked open the door, peeking her head outside. It was quiet again.

"Hello?" Lou said quietly, looking around the perimeter. She saw nothing, but there was still a nervous energy in the air that was starting to frighten her. The noise turned to skittering, sounding as if it was clawing its way underneath the house. An animal no doubt. Lou snatched a flashlight from the drawer by the door and headed outside. She was usually not the type of person to go chasing after things. It generally stirred up her anxiety too much. But something was pushing her that night.

As she made her way out into the drizzle, she heard the door snap shut behind her. Lou ignored it at first, going to investigate the noise. When she rounded the corner, she flashed the light into the darkness and spotted two raccoons that had knocked over the trash cans that sat against her house. The light and Lou's approaching footsteps were enough to scare them off across the backyard. Lou watched them disappear in the bushes. There was no doubt they'd be back, but at least she'd solved the mystery of the noise.

Lou made her way back around the corner and up the steps straight to the side door. When she'd gotten the screen door open, she pushed into the door and was surprised when she slammed into it, and it hadn't budged. Lou jiggled at the handle, realizing that it was locked. Tight.

Every ounce of the blood in Lou's body went instantly ice cold. Her breathing accelerated, and the entire world began to spin like she was on a carnival ride. Lou pushed into the door again. Nothing. It was locked. She was locked out. Thunder rumbled noisily overhead, and the rain picked up a little.

Maybe the front door was open. Lou darted around to the front of the house, feeling her insides quivering. What if she had to stay out here all night? Had she left the stove on in the kitchen? What if the whole house burnt down to the ground? She could likely stay with her brother, but this house had meant so much to their family...

Lou raced onto the front porch and felt herself fall into the front door. Her hands were damp, sweat mixed with the rainwater. She jiggled the handle, but much like the side door, it was locked tight. Her chest constricted. Every muscle in her neck and shoulders tightened to a terribly painful degree. The vein in between her eyes was thumping so hard, it was causing a massive headache.

What was she going to do? How could she have been so stupid?

Somehow Lou managed to make it back to the side entrance of the house. By then, she couldn't find her breath. Her entire body was shaking. Instead of standing, she slouched against the side of the house, resting her head between her legs. Begging herself to think. There had to be something she wasn't remembering. Some way to get inside.

Another rustle came, and Lou's head jerked up. Lightning flashed again, and Lou jerked in place. Out of nowhere, a blur of white came whizzing through the darkness. It darted up the side steps, and Lou felt herself pushing back into the side of the house, terrified. A loud woof filled the air, and the dog slid to a halt right in front of her.

Lou stared into the night, realizing she was looking straight at Caspian's face in front of her. The dog was drenched. She stared blankly, trying to figure out what was going on. Maybe she was still asleep, just dreaming. Eventually, she came to. "What are you doing here, buddy?"

Another moving creature came from the darkness, inching up toward the door. When Lou turned her attention on it, she saw the petite blonde, with the pastel pink rain slicker standing in the driveway. Alice Gray was staring at her, looking rather concerned. "Lou?"

"What are you doing here?" Lou asked, getting to her feet despite her legs still feeling wobbly.

"I could ask you the same question," Alice replied. Just as she did, another crash of thunder came, and with it, the downpour of rain. She ran up the steps to stand next to Lou, under the small awning by the side door. They stared at one another while the white German Shepherd sat at their feet. "Why are you standing outside? Do you still live here?"

"I locked myself out," Lou replied while nodding, still feeling the terrible thudding in her chest. For some reason, Alice being there had eased her anxiety a little. Alice reached out, opening the screen door and wiggling the handle much like Lou had done.

"I guess you did," Alice said in agreement. They both stared at one another for a long moment before Alice looked away, down along the side of the house. Before Lou could ask, she took off down the side, pushing against windows as she walked. Lou watched her curiously, through the pelting rain. Finally, she jogged to catch up with her, Caspian following along at her side. Alice turned to look behind her. "I was thinking maybe one of your windows might be open.

They walked around the entire perimeter checking, but to no avail. Once they'd reached the front of the house, Alice looked up toward the second story windows. "Do you have a ladder in your garage?" She'd raised her voice a little, likely to be audible over the pouring rain.

Lou stared at her confused, but finally nodded. The pair made their way over to the small detached garage in the driveway and worked together to roll up the door. Lou disappeared into the garage, dragging out a ladder for Alice. They made their way back around the front of the house with it. Once they'd set it up against the side of the roof, Alice started to make her way up. Lou stopped her a few steps in. "What are you doing?"

"Trying to get us inside," Alice argued, slipping from her grasp. Meanwhile, Caspian was staring intently. Alice scampered up the ladder through the pouring rain, straight to one of the three windows in the front of the second story of the house. She tugged at the farthest one, and sure enough it slid open. Lou watched in awe as she disappeared through the window. A minute later, she appeared at the front door, throwing it open. Lou and Caspian made their way up the steps of the porch and straight to the doorway.

"How did you—" Lou stared, and Alice's face erupted into a smile.

"You don't remember sneaking in through that window in high school?"

The memory of their late-night date flashed back into Lou's mind. What a date it had been, too. It was the first time Lou and Alice had slept together, under a clear and starry Portland sky, on a blanket in the park. Lou would have stayed the entire night but knew she'd be grounded for life by her father if she didn't return home. So, instead, Alice had dropped her off rather late and Lou had snuck in through the window that her brother had left open.

Every piece of that memory rushed through Lou, like the rain torrent had washed over her outside. It was warm and inviting and as perfect as it had been all those years ago. The memory caused her to take pause, and by the time she came back to the present, she realized Alice had been staring at her. Caspian was waiting patiently at her feet. "Are you going to come inside or what?" Alice asked, though she was still smiling.

Lou headed inside, the dog trailing behind her at her feet, tail wagging and tongue hanging out of his mouth. "Sit," Lou said immediately, noticing the buckets of water that the dog was leaking onto the floor. Caspian sat promptly and Lou disappeared down the hall to the linen closet. She fetched towels for each of them, and when she returned handed one off to Alice. The moment their fingers came together, an electric shock radiated through Lou, from top to bottom. The warmth of Alice's skin beneath her fingertips was intoxicating. She almost didn't want to move away, but she shook her head free of the lingering thoughts.

"I'm glad you showed up," Lou finally said, as she dried off her hair. Alice removed the rain slicker she was wearing and began toweling off her short blonde locks. Once she finished, she hung the towel on the coatrack by the door and turned her attention back to Caspian. While Lou squeezed the excess water from her hair, she watched Alice towel the dog down. She then went into the kitchen and returned the kettle to the stove. When she turned back around, Alice was staring at her.

"You live here? How is your dad?" Alice asked. The mention of her father sent a pang of sadness through Lou. She hesitated for a minute, unsure if she wanted to answer, but it was clearly written all over her face. "Oh, Lou... He didn't... I'm so sorry, I shouldn't have asked."

"It's okay," Lou looked down at Alice who was still drying the dog. "He died a few years ago."

"From the Huntington's?" Alice asked. They'd had to put him in a nursing home shortly before he passed away, but the disease had progressed so quickly. Far quicker than she or Stephen had expected it to. Lou nodded, and Alice's face dropped further. "I'm so sorry."

"I know," Lou said, offering a small smile of gratitude. The kettle squawked on the stove and Lou went to fetch it. "You still like mint tea?" Lou looked over her shoulder at Alice, who was getting to her feet as Caspian wandered off down the hallway.

Lou fixed her a cup and brought it over to the kitchen table, just as Alice had sat down. She sat down across from her, taking a sip of the tea she had made a little while earlier. It had cooled substantially, but still tasted good nonetheless. "Steve didn't want the house, so I decided to take it. It's been in our family for so long, we didn't have the heart to sell it." Before Lou, it had belonged to her parents, and her grandmother before that. Three generations.

"Makes sense," Alice said, sipping on her tea. They stared at each other for a moment before Lou's attention dropped back down to her drink. She stirred the tea bag around briefly before she heard Alice clear her throat. Caspian had come to lay down in the middle of the kitchen floor, watching the pair. Lou turned her attention back to Alice. "Are you okay?"

The question caught Lou off-guard, and she wasn't sure what she meant. "What do you mean?"

"You just looked like you were having an anxiety attack—" Alice started, but looked hesitant to continue. Lou couldn't help but smile a little at the thoughtfulness.

"I'm okay," she reassured Alice, taking another sip of tea before she continued. "I'm just glad you showed up. I wouldn't have thought to go through that window." Lou likely wouldn't have been able to make it up the ladder. Her fear would have gotten the best of her. Alice had always been the fearless one between them. "So, thank you."

Alice smiled and took another sip of her drink. Both of their attentions then turned to Caspian, who had closed his eyes and was dozing on the floor. They sat in silence for a few minutes, enjoying the patter of the rain outside and the rumbling thunder. Lou loved the rain but was grateful to be inside her house. When she finally turned her attention back to Alice, the blonde was looking straight at her, still smiling softly. "What?" Lou asked.

"You just seem content," Alice noted. "And I'm glad."

Lou sat thoughtfully on that comment for a minute, not replying. Was she content? She supposed so. "For the most part. There's still things I miss." Lou hadn't realized what she'd said until it was out of her mouth. Had she meant it in relation to Alice? Probably, the more she thought about it. Her words caused her to go silent again.

Alice had finished the last mouthful of her tea and sat the mug back on the table. "My dad is waiting on me," she noted, getting up from her seat. "I probably should get back home before he gets worried." Alice snapped the leash back on Caspian and then Lou followed her as she wound her way around the kitchen and to the side door.

"Do you want me to drive you home?" Lou said, looking out the window. It was still drizzling lightly but the storm appeared to have subsided. When Alice shook her head, Lou plucked a black umbrella off the counter and handed it to her. "Well, at least take this then."

"Thanks for the tea," Alice said, taking the umbrella graciously.

"Thanks again for rescuing me," Lou said, offering up a smile. "You seem to do that a lot."

Alice laughed, brushing a wet strand of blonde hair from her eyes. She didn't reply but bobbed her head by way of acknowledgement. Lou held open the side door for her, and Alice stepped out onto the porch once she'd pulled the hood of her rain slicker over her head. She turned to look at Lou again, just as Caspian headed out the door. "Have a good night."

"You too," Lou replied, watching Alice as she made her way down the walkway and onto the sidewalk, until she'd disappeared behind the bushes that lined the street, with Caspian at her side.

———

"Let me know how that works for you," Lou said to Eric and Melissa, the parents of Robbie, a ten-year-old who was working with Turtle, a black lab. Lou had just gotten through showing them a technique to help Robbie, since Tammy was busy elsewhere. "Have a good afternoon guys. See you next class."

When Lou turned her focus back to the other side of the room, she noticed Anna and Alice working with Caspian on obedience training, most of which they'd learned that morning. Sitting, staying, and coming when called. Alice mostly moderated while Anna practiced giving commands. Lou watched for a few minutes, admiring them working together, and how patient Caspian had gotten with Anna.

Finally, Lou approached, toting a handful of treats. She squatted down next to Anna. "I brought you some more treats." Anna held her hands out and Lou dumped them into her palms. Once she'd safely gathered them, Anna stuffed them in her pockets and handed a few to Caspian. "Here you go, Caspian." The dog took them from her hand gently.

"Did you get what you needed to get done?" Alice asked, looking at Lou.

Lou nodded. "How's she doing?" She looked at Anna, who was trying to get the dog to sit again, successfully. Once he had, and Anna had felt him obey her, she handed off a handful of treats. "He'll keep eating those until he can't walk, if you aren't careful."

Alice laughed, and Lou laughed right alongside her. It felt good to laugh with her. Normal, even. Familiar. When they fell silent again, they looked at one another. "Thanks for helping us today."

"It's no problem, Alice," Lou said. "It's my job." She'd said it before thinking about it too much, and Alice's facial expression gave the impression that she thought it was a weird reply. But she was still smiling. Lou started to pick up around the room, and Alice joined in while Anna played with Caspian. They worked together to clear up toys and equipment, putting them into plastic bins and storage containers. Once they'd finished, Alice helped lead Anna to the row of benches that lined the far wall of the building. Lou followed behind and they all sat together.

Caspian fell in front of Anna's feet, curled up. Alice was watching Lou quietly when she finally paid attention. Lou studied her for a long moment, unsure of what to say. "What?"

"Nothing," Lou said, and Alice gave her a look that read she didn't believe her at all. An all too familiar look. Lou smiled. "I'm just glad to see you again is all."

"Me, too," Alice said thoughtfully, and there was a flutter in Lou's chest that she hadn't felt in a long time. A warm feeling that spread from the middle of her chest outward and wrapped itself around her like a warm blanket. Alice paused for a moment before she continued, "Would you want to come and get something to eat with Anna and me?" Anna looked up, hearing her mother talking about food, but didn't say anything. "We could go to Goose Hollow Inn."

How many years had it been since Lou had heard that name? The last time she'd been inside that particular establishment was with Alice on her arm. The restaurant was a local favorite, close by where the two had lived. It had been a popular hangout for them during college and high school, where they'd get early morning breakfasts before school, or late-night dinners for study sessions.

Lou's feelings on the matter must have been evident on her face. As surprised and flattered by the offer as she was, it also sent her into a spiral of panic. Lou could feel herself shutting down, her brain unable to process her thoughts. Instead she stood there silent, heart pounding in her chest and a ringing forming in her ears. "Oh, I shouldn't have asked—" Alice trailed off.

"No, no," Lou said, standing up from her seat. "It was very nice of you to offer…" She trailed off, unsure of what to say. "I just have some things I need to take care of is all."

Alice's face fell in disappointment and it made Lou's heart sink a little further in her chest. She felt horrible, fighting desperately to take back what she'd said. Lou wanted nothing more than to spend her evening in Alice's company. But the feelings she was having… Lou's feelings weren't platonic. They were full of heady desires and longing unlike anything she'd felt in a long time. Lou wanted Alice, far more than she cared to admit in that moment.

There was nothing to want. Alice was a taken woman with a family, a woman Lou had lost years ago from stupid mistakes. Stupid mistakes that would haunt her to her dying day.

"No problem," Alice said, she blinked quickly looking as if she was fighting tears. She got to her feet and helped Anna up. Lou dropped down to pick up Caspian's leash from the floor. "Maybe another time?"

Lou nodded, and trailed around them to the front door. She could hear Alice following behind her. The door propped open, and

Lou stood beside it, with Caspian at her leg. "Have a good afternoon, Alice. Bye, Anna."

"Bye, Lou," Anna said, as she gripped onto her mother's arm. Alice gave her a brief wave and quickly disappeared out the door.

As soon as Lou turned around from the door, Tammy was standing behind her, watching her curiously. She had Jesse's dog, Phil, on a leash beside her. He was sitting patiently, looking up at her. "What?" Lou asked, shutting the door behind her.

"You should have gone with her," Tammy said, nodding at the door.

"You heard that?" Lou sighed, slouching back into one of the plush gray cushioned benches by the doorway. "I forgot you're a good eavesdropper." Lou ran her fingers over Caspian's head, pondering for a moment before she spoke again. "I can't go down that road again, Tammy. Not after what happened before."

"It was just a meal," Tammy noted. "You're putting too much thought into it."

Was she? Lou wasn't sure what to think about that. Maybe she was. Especially if Alice was already a taken woman. Alice had too much integrity to cheat on her husband. Perhaps all she'd wanted was just to spend time with Lou again, like they had before.

"I don't know if I can," Lou argued.

"You won't know if you don't try," Tammy said.

I t had been several years since Lou had even driven by Goose Hollow Inn. The building was a red-clay brick, the hue varying from russet to autumnal browns. It had a roughness that reminded Lou of rocks upon the beach, the kind that were made so pretty by the barnacles that clung to it. The mortar had been there for many-a-year, holding the bricks together as they were, standing tall.

The building was weathered on the outside but had a magical charm about it on the inside. It very much resembled a pub, with plush leather booths and a bar that wrapped around its length. Lou scanned the room, searching for Alice's distinctive blonde hair.

A hostess caught her attention. "Can I help you?"

"I'm just looking for a friend," Lou replied, stepping into the building. She scanned down the aisles, until she'd scoured the entire room. At the far end of the restaurant she could make out Alice's short cropped blonde hair, and her daughter sitting beside her. Lou waved to thank the hostess before she started off down the row of booths. She hadn't made it but a few feet forward when she realized Alice wasn't alone. Sitting across from Alice was a man and his daughter. Lou recognized him from the training class. Cooper, if she remembered rightly. They'd met briefly the first day of classes. He and Alice were laughing about something, but over the commotion of the restaurant, Lou had no idea what exactly.

Lou stared for a minute, feeling a lump forming in her throat. Finding it hard to breathe. Thoughts of Alice's husband Jeremy flashed through her mind, wondering why he hadn't come with Alice and Anna. Jeremy and Lou had met each other a handful of times when they'd all been in college. He was one of Alice's closest friends, and Alice's parents had loved him dearly. But they had never been that close. Lou felt a flicker of annoyance that had come from nowhere. Was she jealous of them? Lou suddenly wished it was her at that table, and not Cooper. It had been a while since she'd felt such a feeling, and it felt rather foreign. It was so overwhelming that she couldn't stand there for long.

Lou made her way back into the parking lot, leaning against the brick exterior, letting the cool, weathered rock fall against her. She stared out at the parking lot that was still rather busy, watching as people made their way inside of the building. Goose Hollow Inn had always been a popular place amongst Portlanders.

Finally, Lou dug through her pockets for her phone. She dialed the one person she needed in that moment. It rang once, twice, and then he answered.

"Walty, you want some food?"

Chapter Ten

"How long have you been teaching?"

Alice had just taken a sip of water, looking down at the Goose Hollow Inn menu, lost in thought. It had been years since she'd been here, and the last time she had it was with Lou. The idea that she was here again with another person left her feeling a little guiltier than she'd expected. And far too focused on Lou for her liking. Following Lou's earlier rejection, she had impulsively decided to cash in on that rain check and was now sitting down to dinner with Cooper and his daughter.

"Oh, sorry," Alice shook her head and returned to the conversation. "Six years now," she replied. "My mom and grandmother were both teachers, so I just followed in their footsteps."

"And you said you teach English?" Cooper asked, taking a sip of his own sweet tea. Alice watched him drink it, thinking about her father and how he always enjoyed sweet tea on hot days. "Who's your favorite author?" Alice looked over at Anna, who was busy conversing with Jesse across the table. She smiled briefly, pleased her daughter had made a friend.

"Oh, that's a tricky one—" Alice pondered for a minute, trying to think of a good answer. "I could tell you some of the classics, because I've read them all so many times now I could recite them verbatim." Cooper laughed, and it caused Alice to smile. "But can I be honest?"

"Of course," Cooper replied, still smiling.

"I *really* love the Harry Potter series," Alice shrugged. "But don't tell my students that."

"I love Harry Potter!" Jesse interrupted their conversation, which caused laughter around the table. Alice was just about to reply when she looked up from the table. In the aisle, she watched as Lou swiftly turned on a heel heading back outside. She wondered if Lou had seen her with Cooper and fled the building because of it. If it hadn't been for Anna sitting beside her, Alice might have gotten up to follow her out. Instead, she watched as Lou disappeared, unable to stop her.

"Are you okay?" Cooper asked and Alice watched him turn to look down the restaurant where she'd been looking.

"I'm fine," Alice said, shaking her head and forcing a small smile. "So, Harry Potter…"

"What house are you?" Jesse asked.

————

Alice curled her bare toes on the freshly cut grass of the field in Troutdale. After the morning's monsoon, it was pleasantly cool, refreshing even. She crouched down to run her hands through the grass, watching as it danced around her fingers. When she looked up, Caspian had dropped a bright green ball at Alice and Anna's feet. Alice handed it to Anna, who flung her arm behind her shoulder and tossed it forward, sending the ball flying in a sideways direction.

Caspian took off through the fields and down the hill, to the point that Alice couldn't make out where he'd run off to. They waited for a minute before Alice picked up her daughter from the ground and propped her against her waist, walking outward to where she'd last seen him.

"Caspian," she called, but there was no sign of him anywhere.

If he'd run off again… Alice pushed the thought from her head. "Come, Caspian!"

There was a rustle in the bushes down the hill. Alice waited patiently for a few seconds until a blur of fur darted out. What was once a white dog was covered from head to toe in thick russet colored mud, and bits of sticks and brush. Alice groaned.

"What's wrong, Mama?" Anna asked, and Alice couldn't help but laugh.

"Caspian's gone and gotten himself dirty," Alice replied as the dog approached them. There wasn't enough time to take the dog home to get clean, nevertheless explain his disheveled appearance to her mother, who would undoubtedly have a fit.

She looked down the road, where the Portland Guide Dog Association sat about a block away, deciding that if anyone knew what to do with the muddy dog, it had to be Lou. She snapped the leash to his collar and grasped Anna's hand lightly. "You ready?" Anna nodded and the three of them took off down the sidewalk toward the building.

There was still a half hour until classes started. Alice came to a halt right outside the door, wondering what she would do with Caspian, instead of dragging him through the building. She was just about to tell Anna to hold onto him when the door opened. Surprisingly, Lou was on the other side. She blinked, coming to an abrupt stop. "You're here early—oh," her eyes had diverted down to Caspian. A bright, hearty laugh escaped her. "Wow. You can't seem to keep out of trouble, can you?" Caspian barked in reply, which made Lou laugh even harder.

Alice fell captive to that laughter. It reeled her in, tangling her in its clutches. She found herself laughing right alongside her. "Can you help me, please?" Alice pleaded. "I don't know what to do."

"We'll clean him up," Lou promised. "Let's take him around back though."

A tug at Alice's summer dress brought her attention down to her daughter. "Mama."

"Hey, Anna," Lou squatted down to meet her, and Anna's head tilted in her direction. "Would you want to come help Tammy with the dogs for a few minutes?" The expression on Anna's face seemed to indicate she was rather excited at the prospect. "I can take her?" Lou looked up to Alice, and she nodded her agreement. The way Lou was with her daughter made Alice's heart swell about three sizes larger in her chest. Alice watched from the doorway as Lou led Anna inside, weaving her over to Tammy. She looked as if she was explaining something for a minute, and Tammy looked back to wave at Alice. Then Lou came back to meet Alice at the doorway. "Let's go deal with the rascal."

The three weaved their way around the outside of the building to the back. They cut through a gravel yard and up a concrete ramp to a back doorway. Lou opened the door and let Alice inside first with Caspian. They were in a kennel area, an expanse of tall and long metal cages lining the walls. Some housed a few dogs, who greeted them with friendly barks as they walked by. Across the room was a row of showers, with plastic enclosures that acted as a gate in front.

Alice handed off Caspian to Lou, who brought him straight into the shower and locked the enclosure behind him. "This makes it a little easier for us to shower the dogs," Lou explained. "Sometimes they don't want anything to do with the shower. Lucky for us, Caspian likes a good bath. Don't you?" Caspian barked in agreement, his tail thumping on the floor. Meanwhile, Lou handed Alice a waterproof apron to cover the front of her yellow summer dress hoping it would catch any surplus spray.

As Lou unhooked the shower head from the wall, she started the water. She handed it to Alice, smiling. "You dirtied him, you bathe him."

"He dirtied himself," Alice argued, but smiled back at the same time.

"Whatever you say," Lou replied, pulling dog shampoo from the top of the wall inside the shower. "Just make sure not to get water in his ears. They don't like that much."

"No water in the ears. Got it." Alice said, before taking a hold of the sprayer and starting to wet Caspian down. His fur flattened against his body, but he looked like he was enjoying himself. Lou squatted down beside Alice, running her hands over his fur to clean off some of the mud. They were close together now, closer than they had been in nearly a decade. So close, that when Lou turned to look at her briefly, Alice could feel her warm breath against her skin. She swallowed deeply and returned to what she was doing.

Lou was busy pouring shampoo on the back of the dog, who sat patiently and calmly. Once she'd finished, Alice dropped the shower head gently on the ground and helped Lou lather up Caspian's white fur. They worked together in tandem, Lou scrubbing his lower half, while Alice worked on his upper half. The two were quiet for a minute, until Alice felt Lou's attention on her again. Alice finally broke the silence. "I saw you at Goose Hollow Inn," she said, briefly looking at Lou. "I didn't think you'd come."

"I didn't either," Lou said, combing her fingers through Caspian's fur. Alice watched her work, entranced by the dancing of her fingers. "I didn't want to interrupt your dinner with Cooper."

"You could have come," Alice argued. "Cooper and I are just friends. His daughter and Anna really get along." Lou's body stiffened as she leaned back against the side of the shower.

"Can I ask you a question?" Lou's voice had grown surprisingly serious.

"Sure," Alice replied, running water over the front of Caspian's chest. The mud was still caked on pretty heavily and it would take a few good washes to get it out completely. She filled her hands with shampoo again and ran her fingers through his fur while she waited on Lou to answer.

"What happened with you and Jeremy?"

The question felt like a truck that had come out of nowhere. It hit Alice harder than she had anticipated, and almost made her feel dizzy in a way. She shook her head, finally seeming to recover. "How did you—"

"You aren't wearing a wedding ring," Lou noted. "So, I just kind of assumed…"

At first, she wasn't sure if she wanted to answer, or to tell her it wasn't any of her business. But for some reason she felt the urge to be candid about it, and looked back at her. "We separated. A year ago."

Lou looked surprised, to say the least. "Separated? As in divorced?" Alice nodded. There was concern in the way Lou was looking at her. Alice knew she was going to dig. Deep. "Can I ask why?"

Alice took a breath. "It was me," she explained. "I've just always thought of Jeremy as a great friend. I don't know. I wasn't there anymore… I didn't feel like me." The expression on Lou's face was unreadable. At first Alice wasn't sure if she'd gone too far in explaining, but suddenly she felt Lou's hand wrap around hers, gently.

"Sometimes the heart wants what the heart wants," Lou said.

"Sometimes it does," Alice agreed. She smiled softly and they sat looking at one another for a long minute. Alice felt Lou's grip tighten slightly on her hand, squeezing it. Alice let out a soft sigh, closing her eyes briefly. She'd missed this. Missed them, together, like they used to be. She hadn't realized how much she'd missed being with Lou until that moment. When she opened her eyes, Lou was still staring at her intently. Alice watched as she drew in closer and wondered for a second if she might pull away in panic. Instead, she stood frozen in place, wondering if Lou's mouth would taste as sweet as it had all those years ago.

Alice felt a light smack on her cheek, as a hand full of bubbles landed there. Lou let out a cheery laugh as Alice tried to regain her composure. As soon as she'd realized what had happened, she laughed too, shaking her head free of the thoughts that she'd been having.

Caspian let out a soft bark that broke both of their focus. They went back to work, finishing cleaning him. When he came out of the shower, the two toweled him off and Alice snapped his collar back around his neck. "Let's go," Lou said, nodding toward the front of the building. "We're gonna be late."

Alice chuckled and gave Caspian the command to follow along. Just before they reached the door, Lou turned back to face her. She didn't speak for a moment and Alice wondered just what she had wanted.

"I was wondering if you'd like to come to Steve's birthday party tomorrow," Lou asked. It had been so long since she'd thought about Lou's brother, his birthday had escaped her. "It's only if you want to. But I'm sure he and the family would love to see you again. You can bring Anna if you want."

Alice couldn't help but smile. "That'd be nice, actually. I could use a night out."

"Great," Lou said, looking pleased. "It's a date, then."

———

The faint drumming of Alice's fingers against a Tupperware container filled the otherwise quiet car. She sat in the driveway of an old Portland Foursquare house that was painted a shade of trout gray with cream white trim. It was bright and cheerful outside, a perfect day for a barbecue. Inside the blue handled dish was freshly made southern potato salad. It was a staple food at her parents' table growing up, and her mother's prized secret recipe that she'd only recently learned. It was Alice's favorite dish to make for gatherings like this.

Alice had arrived early, at the insistence of Lou, who wanted her to mingle with her family before the rest of the guests arrived. Seeing Steve and Kelly and their daughter again was making it very difficult to get out of the car, nevertheless get up the stairs to the house.

This was all happening so fast. It felt as if the past eight years had just disappeared. As if things had picked up just the way they were before. And unresolved feelings were bubbling to the surface that Alice hadn't felt in years. She missed those stirring emotions, more than she cared to admit.

But at the same time, the feelings petrified her.

After a long final deep breath, Alice worked up the nerve to exit the car and make her way up the cobblestone path, up seven steps, to the front porch. Three stories, with a walk out porch on the second level and an attic room up top. It was a marvelous looking house. There was a smooth, cushioned Amador rocking chair that sat out front. Alice recognized it as Adam's chair. She remembered the day it had come, shipped all the way from Nicaragua after he'd gotten back from a trip there. It was older now, a little aged, but it brought back memories of days sitting with Lou on her front porch—Lou in a hammock and Alice rocking in the chair. Memories that were distant now.

It took a minute, but Alice finally rang the doorbell. As she waited, she shifted her weight from one foot to the other, fiddling with the container in her hands. Before long, the door cracked open.

Lou stood inside, and the sight of her caused Alice's breath to hitch in her throat. The girl who was always adorned in T-shirts and jeans had dressed up for the day. Alice couldn't recall the last time she'd seen Lou in a blouse but thought maybe it had been for a presentation in college. The striped blue and green crew neck shirt was conservative, but the cut accentuated the slight curve of her hips and her long slender arms. Lou's gorgeous red hair had been piled up on her head and little pieces hung lose framing her face.

Alice's tongue drew in one delicate motion across her lips, feeling rather parched in that moment. Lou was smiling at her, drawing the door open farther. "You came," she said, ushering her inside.

"I did," Alice replied, shifting the bowl around in her hands, which were now starting to perspire. A cool burst of air-conditioning greeted her, which was refreshing after the heat outside. "You look nice," Alice noted, doing her best to be as casual as possible.

"It's been a while since you've seen me in a blouse," Lou's face was still stretched in a smile, reading Alice's mind. "Enjoy it. It'll be the last time you see me in one until next year." Lou had said it so nonchalantly, that the implication of her statement had obviously not registered with her like it had for Alice.

The woman was assuming there was a 'next year,' whatever that meant.

94

Alice shook it off, thrusting the bowl of potato salad in Lou's direction.

"Your mom's?" Lou guessed, and Alice nodded. A happy sigh escaped her. "I can't guarantee that this won't all be gone by the time everyone gets here."

"That's okay." Alice finally broke into a smile of her own. "I made it especially for you." She couldn't see Lou's reaction as she had turned and was already walking down the hallway. Alice followed, a nervous mess. As they walked, she admired the photos on the wall of Steve and his family. Pictures from family vacations to scenic and tropical places. The Grand Canyon and San Francisco were featured. They looked very well-traveled, to say the least. Alice imagined Steve had taken over his father Adam's business and that he was well off.

They turned the corner into the kitchen and Alice saw a woman working at the counter, her back turned. Lou cleared her throat, and the woman turned around on her heel. The nerves Alice was feeling over seeing Lou's sister-in-law and brother again were overwhelming, especially after how things had been left the last time that they had seen one another. Alice had left Lou, after all. Kelly hadn't aged a day, with the exception, perhaps, of a few stray wrinkles. "Oh my gosh, Alice!" Kelly dropped her utensils on the counter and rushed to meet her. Alice felt the warm, friendly embrace of someone who she had once seen as family. "Stephen! Come see who's here." Kelly had called for him over her shoulder, before turning back to Alice. "Wow, you look beautiful. I love your short hair."

Alice felt her cheeks glowing as her smile spread across her face. Before she could speak, Steve Pearson had made his way through the glass sliding doors at the far end of the kitchen. Alice could never get over how similar he and Lou looked.

"Well, if it isn't little Ally." Stephen's smile was nearly as big as Alice's. They made their way toward each other, and Alice folded herself into his arms. While the siblings looked much alike, both having fiery red hair and blue eyes, Stephen was much broader and thicker than Lou's tiny frame, but his additional size made for an excellent hug. Alice sighed, enjoying the familiarity of him again.

Surprised that he had been so inviting after everything that had happened.

Alice was at a loss for words seeing Lou's brother after so many years. Lou stood beside him, beaming as they reconnected for the first time in nearly a decade. Alice was an only child and Steve had been as close to a sibling as anyone could be. It had been nearly as terrible separating from the Pearson's as it had been from Lou herself. "It's so good to see you," Alice let out a relieved breath, finally allowing herself to break into a genuine smile. "Happy Birthday." He was forty now. How quickly time had passed, Alice could barely believe it.

"You too," Stephen said, squeezing her shoulder. Lou looked just about as happy as Alice had seen her since they'd reconnected, and truthfully she felt the same way. "And thanks for coming. How have you been? Lou told us you were in Portland, and I couldn't believe it." Alice was surprised at how welcoming Lou's family were being. She had been worried that they were going to be hostile following how things had been left between her and Lou but instead, they seemed as normal as ever, embracing her as much now as they had then. Their cheery demeanor was rubbing off on Alice, easing her nerves.

"Just staying busy teaching," Alice replied, following Steve and Kelly to the couch. Meanwhile, Lou had disappeared down the hallway. "I live in Seattle now with my daughter, Anna."

"Lou mentioned you had a daughter," Kelly replied. "She wasn't sure if you were going to bring her or not."

"She's having a day with grandma," Alice admitted, though there had been a variety of reasons Anna hadn't come. Including the fact that Alice was spending time with her ex-girlfriend. She wasn't quite ready for her daughter to be let into that part of her life. "It's been a while since they've seen each other."

"I'm glad you came," Kelly said, still beaming at her. "It's so wonderful to see you again." Wonderful was an understatement. It just felt right. Like she'd never left.

When Alice looked up again, Lou had come back into the room toting what looked to be nearly a teenage version of Kelly. Alice's eyes went wide when she saw her. Rebecca sat down sheepishly beside her mother. "Wow, have you ever grown," Alice breathed.

"Twelve this year," Kelly replied, wrapping an arm around her daughter. "Rebecca, you probably don't remember, but this is Alice. She and Lou used to date a long time ago. You were a little squirt then."

Alice had always loved how naturally it came to Lou's family to be open about their relationship. They'd never been embarrassed or hesitant to admit it to anyone, including Rebecca, who looked curious to say the least. "Don't call me squirt, Mom," Rebecca said, rolling her eyes. "Nice to meet—I mean, see you again," Rebecca extended her hand and Alice shook it. The kid had a firm grip, a lot like her father's.

"You, too," Alice agreed.

"Alice used to come over all the time," Kelly mused. "She and Lou were attached at the hip. We loved having them over. Remember when we used to live in that little apartment?" Rebecca grinned.

The place downtown, Alice remembered it herself. It had been so many years ago now. A small, two-bedroom apartment, right down the street from where she and Lou had lived throughout college. They'd spent nearly every weekend with Stephen and Kelly, playing board games, grilling out, watching movies…

"We had a lot of fun back then, didn't we?" Stephen thought out loud. Alice agreed, casting her gaze for a moment on Lou, who was watching her with a smile. "I thought you two were going to be together until you both croaked."

"Do you remember Monopoly nights?" Kelly asked. "Lou always won no matter how hard we tried…"

"It was because she always managed to buy Park Place and Boardwalk and built all those hotels…" Stephen chuckled and Lou tossed a throw pillow at him which he caught one handed. "Don't say it wasn't true, Lou."

"Maybe if you guys didn't gang up on me," Lou was grinning. "I couldn't help it if Alice always had bad luck with rolling and landed on me all the time." Alice gave her a dirty look, which caused Lou to erupt into laughter. "It's okay, you still beat us all at Texas Hold'em."

Alice sighed, a smile still stretched across her face as she relaxed back into the couch. She felt content as she listened to Lou and her family reminisce about the old days that were still fresh in her mind and seemed like they'd only happened yesterday. Days she wouldn't have traded for the world. She felt relaxed and at peace, for the first time in a very long time. She was enjoying herself and letting lose.

Stephen and Kelly's friends began to arrive shortly after. While Alice was no stranger to mingling with new people, she was grateful that Lou stuck by her most of the evening. "This is my friend Alice," Lou would introduce her. It felt good to be 'friends' with Lou again. She'd changed so much these past eight years. She had relaxed a lot and become far more open than she used to be. It also came as a surprise that Lou was so sociable now; back when they had dated Lou always wanted to stay home whilst Alice was the social butterfly of the two. Now Alice could see that it came almost naturally to her, and Alice felt like the shy one to a certain extent.

"How long have you and Lou known one another?" Alice had just finished her hamburger when David, one of Stephen's friends from work, inquired. She gave a quick glance to Lou, smiling.

"I've known her half my life," Alice admitted. It was crazy to think that now. It felt like she'd known her for forever. "We met in high school." That day on the bus flashed in Alice's mind, when Lou had struck up conversation about the book she'd been reading. Alice had thought she was such a kind person.

She still was a kind person. Lou was smiling at her when Alice turned her attention back to her, and she tucked a piece of her red hair behind her ear before she broke away. "I always copied her homework."

"I think it was the other way around," Lou laughed.

"It must be really nice knowing someone that long," David said. "I don't think I have anyone except family I've known that long."

Alice found herself looking at Lou again, who was staring right back at her. It was hard to break away from her. The fact that she had known her for that long was nice. Seeing her again after all these years was even nicer. Feelings welled up inside of her that were starting to bubble over, and Alice suddenly felt like she might be losing control. She looked down at her watch. "I probably better get going," she said, getting to her feet. "My daughter is waiting at home for me."

When Alice found Stephen and Kelly in the crowd of people, she was engulfed in another hug by Lou's brother. It was tight and full of emotion that overwhelmed every part of Alice. "You come by again before you leave, okay?" Stephen broke away from her, his friendly blue eyes staring intensely at her. They reminded Alice so much of Lou it was breathtaking. Alice nodded just as Kelly wrapped her arms around her.

Lou led them both outside to the front of the house, cutting through the side gate and around to the driveway. They made their way down the driveway to Alice's parked car and stopped once they'd reached the driver's side door. Alice turned to look at Lou, who was smiling at her. "I'm glad you came."

"Me too," Alice replied. There was something about the way Lou was looking at Alice and the feeling was mutual—Alice couldn't *stop* looking at her either. In fact, it was getting rather hard to pull away from her in general. Instead, she found herself drawing closer, until they were barely a few inches apart. Alice could feel the heat of Lou's breath on her cheeks. Lou's hands grasped onto Alice's arms softly, her fingertips brushing against her bare skin.

Alice licked her lips and stared deeply into her eyes. "Lou—"

A clap of thunder ripped the two apart from one another in an instant. As soon as it had, the downpour came, washing over them in a rush of wind and water. They both stood there for a moment, before Lou burst into laughter. "Go, go, get in the car before you get soaked," she said, opening the door for Alice. She slid in quickly and looked up to Lou who was smiling. "See you Monday?"

"See you Monday," Alice agreed, and watched her as she disappeared back inside.

Chapter Eleven

The pitter patter of the rain against the picture window pulled Lou into a perfect bubble. She watched it, transfixed, as it fell against the glass stretched across the front of the building. It was falling like it was a means to wash everything away, like it meant to keep hammering until things began to smudge like a Monet masterpiece. It sounded like the heavens were knocking on the roof and the windows. Inescapable wetness, that made Lou feel chilled, even when she was watching the downpour from inside the building.

Lou's head shook. "Okay, Anna. Let's start again." Her attention went back to Caspian, assessing the dog's attention on Anna. He waited beside the girl, looking prepared to go. "Ready when you are. Alice you'll have to let go of Anna." Alice looked distant and distracted, her hand resting on her daughter's shoulder. She hadn't looked present for the entire class and Lou couldn't understand why. "Alice."

"Oh, sorry," Alice stepped away from her daughter, releasing her hand.

"Forward, Caspian," Anna said, holding on to the dog's harness as he started walking. They had practiced working on several commands at once. While Lou worried about Alice, she kept her focus on her daughter and Caspian. They walked until they had neared a wall and Caspian turned left and made his way around the family who were working with Felicity.

"Good, Anna," Lou reassured her. "Caspian's taking you around the room now. You're going to have to trust him. He'll lead you the right way." Lou took a few steps, keeping up with the girl and the dog. Meanwhile, Alice followed along beside her, quiet and watching.

"Okay, Anna," Lou stopped her after a few more minutes of walking. "Let's stop for the day. Why don't you hang out with Caspian while I talk to your mom?" Alice helped her daughter to sit down in a seat, Caspian coming to sit protectively in front. Anna petted him while Lou reached for Alice's wrist, pulling her aside to a nearby empty corner. "What's going on with you today?"

Alice looked surprised, but remained distracted. "Nothing's wrong, Lou. I'm just tired."

"You've been acting weird," Lou stated. "Did you have a bad time at Steve's?" That evening had been one of the most enjoyable that Lou had experienced in a long time, being with Alice again and seeing her around her family had brought back so many happy memories. There had been an ease between them that hadn't existed in so long. It had been everything that Lou had imagined it would be.

Now, she was worrying if it hadn't been mutual.

"No," Alice almost interrupted her she'd answered so quickly. "That's not it at all."

"What's going on then?" Lou pressed her. "You can talk to me, Alice."

Alice bit her lip, looking lost in thought. "I'm just worried things are moving too fast. After everything that's happened between us. And the way things ended—"

Lou's eyes widened, surprised by her honest answer. She couldn't help but smile in response. "It does feel kind of fast, doesn't it?" Alice nodded. "Well, if it's any consolation, I'm glad you're around again. Regardless of anything else."

"Me too," Alice replied, a small smile spreading across her face.

Lou had a thought, and wondered aloud. "Can I steal you tonight?"

"Steal me?" Alice parroted.

"Just for a few hours. Just me and you. I just want you to come with me somewhere."

"Where?" Alice asked, sounding more confused than ever.

"To my NA meeting."

There was a cool draft floating through the building as Lou led Alice down the concrete steps to the basement of the church. Out of all her meeting places, this was the most familiar, and the meeting she attended most frequently. Something about bringing Alice to this place had her stomach in knots, but she trekked on anyway.

They entered a large room, filled with chairs situated in a circle. The brick wall, painted a cream white, was chipping a little with age and there was a musty smell in the air that had always lingered. Lou took a seat at the far side. It was still empty, both of them having arrived super early. Alice slid in beside her, looking around the room. "You meet in a church?"

Lou nodded. "I don't show up as often as I used to, but yeah. We've met here since I started coming eight years ago."

It took a second, but Alice seemed to realize what that had meant. She didn't push further. When she spoke again, she was looking at a table filled with a spread of food across the way. "Do they have coffee?"

"I think it's from the mom-and-pop coffee place down the street. It's good," Lou noted. Alice seemed pleased with her answer, and got up from her seat, moseying toward the table.

Lou couldn't help but watch the way she walked. The sway of her hips, back and forth. The lightness of her step as she weaved her way through chairs and up to the table. There was another woman, who Lou didn't recognize, fetching coffee. Alice offered a friendly smile and started making small talk as she waited. Lou beamed, watching her. Alice was such a caring and tender person. The kind of person everyone liked.

Lou's thoughts had wandered to where she was staring while Alice made her way back. "What?" Alice asked, as she sat back down beside her.

"Nothing." Lou smiled at her, brushing a strand of red hair from her face. Alice nudged her playfully in the side and Lou couldn't help but laugh.

They chit-chatted for a few minutes while the room began to fill up with people. Alice was watching as they entered, observing each attendee and absorbing every little detail. Lou felt mesmerized by her, captivated by how attentive she was being. How caring and respectful she was to every second of this experience. Her unease, about bringing Alice into this part of her world, settled as a result. This was what she had wanted. It felt right.

In the doorway, Lou could make out the tall frame, with salt-and-pepper hair and green eyes that glistened in the fluorescent glow of the lighting, of Walt. He was scanning the room, looking for Lou she assumed. When Lou got up from her seat, she gave him a small wave. He slowly limped over to meet her and the two shared a brief hug, before Lou turned her attention to Alice. "Walter, there's someone I want you to meet."

"Is this Alice?" Walter asked, grinning. Alice got up from her seat, stretching out a hand, and he shook it without hesitation. "Pleasure to meet you, young lady."

Alice turned her head to Lou, raising a curious brow. "Nice to meet you, too."

"I've heard years and years of stories about you," Walter mused, and Lou could feel her face heating at the comment. "Nice to put a face to all the yabbering."

"Walter's my sponsor," Lou explained. "We've known each other since my first meeting." The comment seemed to make two and two click for Alice, who now looked with deep interest at the elderly man standing before her. "He's a great friend of mine. You want to sit with us?"

Lou's friend smiled and shook his head, waving a hand. "No, no.

You two spend some time together. I'm gonna chat with some folks. Hope you enjoy the meeting." Walter looked at Alice and smiled again. She gave him a quick wave, and he disappeared in the other direction.

When Evan arrived, the moderator of the meeting, they all gathered around after having fetched snacks and coffee. There were at least twenty people in the room now, who had all grown quiet when Evan had gotten to his feet. Alice's eyes zeroed in on him, and Lou stared at her for a moment, before she turned her attention outward.

"Evening, folks," Evan said. "Glad to see we've got our usual's here, and some new faces too. Let's start off by going around the room and introducing ourselves. We'll start with Dave over here." Evan looked to the gentlemen at his left.

The introductions went around the room, until they'd made it to Alice. For a moment, she looked nervous and Lou thought to speak up for her, but she smiled and spoke anyway. "I'm Alice. I'm here to support my friend, Lou." She looked over at Lou, then.

Lou offered a small smile, but inside it had felt like a bullet had ripped through her body. Surprised how much one tiny word had impacted her. Had crushed her spirit. *Friend.* They'd never been just friends. Lou realized, as much as she didn't think she could handle it, she didn't *want* to be just friends with Alice. She couldn't be 'just friends' with Alice.

As the realization sank in, Lou introduced herself and then the last few people in the circle went next.

They recited the Serenity Prayer, like they did at every meeting. It had become second nature to her now and surprisingly, when she looked over at Alice, she could see her mouthing along. *"God, grant me the serenity to accept the things I cannot change—"*

Afterward, they shared their experiences and what had been going on with them over the past few days, weeks, or however long it had been since they'd last attended a meeting. Lou hadn't intended to speak, but she felt an instinctive urge to do so. Even with Alice there, she needed to.

"Hi, everyone," Lou said, standing up from her seat. "I'm Lou, and I'm a recovering addict. I've been clean for eight years." The room applauded and Lou looked down at Alice, who was watching her with bright eyes and her full attention. She turned back toward the room. "I've been having a hard time during these past few weeks. Someone from my past has come back into my life. Someone who was…" Lou paused for a half second before she corrected herself. "Who *is*, important to me." She didn't look back at Alice, preferring to speak to the whole room, even though she knew Alice was listening.

"It's been a big struggle for me," Lou admitted. "This person is a constant reminder of my past. My past as an addict. She's the reason I started coming to meetings. The reason I wanted to stop using. But she was also the one I hurt the most as a result of being an addict."

Lou took a deep breath. "The problem is, I think I still have feelings for her." She couldn't bring herself to look at Alice, unsure if she wanted to see her reaction. "Feelings that I haven't felt in years, but feelings that I kind of enjoy. Feelings I want in my life again."

"I'm not sure what to do with the feelings," Lou admitted. "And that's scaring me."

Lou drifted her gaze to Alice, who she could see was completely focused on her. She sat ramrod straight in her seat, eyes unwavering. There was an unreadable expression on her face, but something told Lou that she wasn't ready to hear what she really wanted to say.

"Anyway, that's how I've been feeling lately. I've just been scared."

"You should talk to them about it," someone across the room suggested.

"Talking helps," Evan confirmed. "Communication is key in any relationship. Especially relationships involving addicts. Admitting your problems is the first step to dealing with them, right?"

Lou nodded, and before she could speak, she heard Alice speak up from beside her. "Who knows? Maybe the person might feel the same way you do."

Chapter Twelve

The building was welcoming from the open front door to the wide hallway. Up on the walls were photographs of dogs, all obviously loved by the people who worked inside. The floor leading into the lobby was of an old-fashioned parquet, a blend of deep homely browns, likely the original flooring of the old mid-century building. The walls were the greens of summer gardens meeting a bold white baseboard.

While the outside was a rundown brick, the inside looked fresh and bright. Cushioned chairs lined the main reception room and a large desk decorated with paw print stickers sat in front of a panoramic window. Alice held her daughter's hand as they made their way inside. It was a little after seven. Lou had surprised them with a trip to the Portland Humane Society after classes that afternoon.

"You volunteer here?" Alice asked, somewhat surprised.

"A couple times a week," Lou replied. Alice wondered how Lou had any time to herself with how busy she was. She supposed she might like it that way. The constant activity keeping her mind from wandering, much like Alice liked teaching for the same reason. Lou had always had an exceptional work ethic, ever since Alice had first met her. "Anna, would you like to see some kittens?" Anna gave an enthusiastic nod and Alice followed Lou through a set of double doors to the back of the building. "She isn't allergic is she?" Alice shook her head.

A large sign on another doorway down a hall read "Cat Room." When Alice looked through the window, after Lou had turned on the lights, she was surprised to find that there were a huge selection of cats and kittens roaming freely inside. "You guys wouldn't want a cat in addition to Caspian, would you? I just went on a police run with a friend of mine to pick up a bunch at an abandoned house."

"You go on *police runs?*" Alice stared at her in disbelief.

"Well, yeah," Lou's face broke into a soft smile. "I help the PPD with cases where animals are involved. The manager of the shelter, Megan, and I generally go on runs together."

Alice didn't reply, just smiled. Lou shoved her body into the door of the cat room and let them all inside. "Go ahead sweetheart," Alice said quietly, letting Anna walk forward. She held on to her hand as they made their way into the room. Once Lou stepped inside, she shut the door behind them.

A dozen cats and various kittens zoomed toward them. Alice helped Anna sit down on the ground. "The ones in this room are pretty friendly," Lou explained, as Alice sat down next to her daughter. An orange and white tabby had come straight up to Anna, rubbing its head against her outstretched fingers. Anna laughed, cupping her hand to pet the animal around its face. Alice watched her briefly, before she turned her attention back on Lou. Cradled in her arms was a gray-blue colored cat with big brown eyes. "This is Binks. He's one of my favorites."

Before Alice could protest, Lou had squatted down beside her and handed him off. "Oh I—" Alice scooped the cat into her arms, and cradled him to her like a baby, belly up, so that he was staring straight up at her. "Oh, aren't you adorable." She sighed, nestling the cat against her chest.

"He's a love bug," Lou agreed, getting back to her feet. Meanwhile, Alice turned her focus back on Anna, who had cats and kittens all around her. Some had crawled onto her lap, whilst some were nudging her to be petted.

"There's so many, Mama," Anna said, in awe.

"Yes there are," Alice agreed. While her fingers scratched on Binks' belly, her eyes scanned the room until she found Lou. She was busy checking food and water bowls, giving careful attention to some of the cats as she went along. Alice watched her in admiration. She was so engaged in what she was doing. It was clear with every single move she made, how incredibly invested she was in these animals. She'd always been invested in animals, ever since Alice had first met her.

Alice watched her blue eyes as they scanned across the room. The way her long fingers combed through an assortment of cats' fur as she trailed by them, and the saunter of her hips as she walked. Everything about her captivated Alice to her very core. Never did she think that Lou would hold her attention again the way she had these past few weeks, but she did, and Alice was at her mercy, whether she liked it or not.

Finally, Lou turned back to Alice, who was still staring. Alice felt heat in her cheeks, embarrassed she'd been so locked on to what the redhead had been doing. Lou didn't seem to mind, shrugging it off with a smile. "You want to go see the dogs?"

"I wanna stay with the kitties," Anna said, sounding rather content.

"Are you going to be okay by yourself for a few minutes?" Alice wondered, though the building was completely empty for the day.

"I'm fine, Mama," Anna replied, hugging a cat in her arms.

"I don't think she'll have a problem," Lou shrugged.

Alice still felt rather nervous, but she decided to trust Lou in this situation. "We'll be back in just a few minutes."

The pair of them left Anna in the room, walking across the hall to the other doorway. This one was marked "Dogs," and didn't have a window like the cat room did. As soon as Lou started to open the door, Alice could hear the chorus of whining inside the room. They stepped inside, and they were surrounded by a sea of kennels, filled with barking dogs.

"It gets a little loud in here," Lou said, as Alice tried to adjust to the noise. The two of them wandered down the row of cages. As they walked side-by-side, Alice felt the gentle graze of Lou's pinky against the side of her hand. She wasn't sure if Lou had meant it or not, but the woman was gone before she had time to think about it. Lou squatted down in front of a kennel by the doorway. "This is Benji. I just found him recently. On a police run."

Alice didn't think she'd get used to the fact that Lou went on actual police runs, but she didn't have much time to think about it. She was too captivated by the scruffy looking reddish brown dog that sat in front of her. "He looks a lot like—"

"Our old dog," Lou said, finishing her thought. "Yeah, I thought so too. Hence the name."

Benji. It made sense. Alice smiled. "He's adorable."

"You want to meet him?" Lou asked, and Alice nodded. She watched as Lou went to fetch a leash and then unlocked the kennel. The dog came out, rather calmly and collected. He sniffed at Alice's hand and then she petted him on top of his head while Lou snapped the leash on him. "Come on. We'll walk him down the hallway so we can keep an eye on Anna."

The simple gesture had Alice's heart tumbling, and a smile stretched across her face so broadly that she thought it might split it. They wandered out into the hall with the dog, shutting the door firmly behind them as they went. Alice went over to check on Anna briefly, who looked a picture of sweetness as she sat on the floor cradling a variety of cats. When she returned, Lou was smiling at her.

"What?" Alice asked, as the pair made their way down the hallway. Lou offered Benji's leash to her, and Alice took it, wrapping it around her hand.

"I always knew you'd be a great mom," Lou shrugged. The comment brought a surge of emotions through Alice that she didn't know was inside of her. Ripping up memories that had been buried within her for years. Lou must have realized by the way her facial expression had shifted that she'd said something wrong. "I didn't mean to upset you…"

"You didn't," Alice reassured her, as they continued down the hallway, Benji sauntering happily between them. She pondered on what to say for a minute, but was surprised when it just came out of her anyway. "I just always expected I'd have a family with you."

"Me too," Lou said, almost immediately in response. They didn't look at one another then, just continued forward. "I'm sorry I ruined that chance for us."

Alice stopped, abruptly, and made eye contact with Lou. Studying her face, with gentle eyes. Taking in all the little details about her that she hadn't forgotten after all these years. The creases around her eyes and the small little dimples in her cheeks. The way she stood, motionless, putting all her weight on her left foot so she was leaning just slightly. All those small, seemingly insignificant details she'd taken for granted for so many years that were blatant now. "You didn't," Alice said firmly, trying to meet Lou's gaze, which seemed to be going in every other direction except on her. "Lou." Before she could stop herself, Alice had reached for her hand, intertwining their fingers together.

God, it had been forever since they'd done that. It took her breath away.

"You were going through something," Alice said. She could feel Lou's thumb grazing the outer side of her hand, which was rather distracting. It was causing all sorts of emotions to whirl through her at a speed that felt way out of control. Alice swallowed, deeply. "You were going through something, and I wasn't there for you. You needed me, and I let you down. And I'm sorry for that."

Lou's expression shifted slightly, looking surprised to say the least by what was coming out of Alice's mouth. Alice, truthfully, was too. She hadn't expected to say what she'd said. "I'm sorry I got scared. I'm sorry I left you when you needed me the most." There was something in Lou's eyes. Something that was making them twinkle more than they normally did. Glisten a more vibrant blue. Alice realized, almost too late, that they were tears.

Hands fell on either side of Lou's face, and Alice stroked away the tears as Lou melted before her like a burning candle. She didn't cry much, just soft, silent tears that rolled down her cheeks. Alice wiped them away with her thumbs, letting her rest there with her eyes closed for a minute. "I'm sorry," she whispered.

"Me too," Lou breathed.

"Mama," Anna's voice broke the silence between them. Alice's hands dropped to her side. Meanwhile, Lou wiped her face with her hands and then reached out to take Benji's leash. As soon as she had, Alice took off down the hallway to the Cat Room door. Through the window, she saw her daughter looking around. Alice came swiftly through the door. Once she'd reached Anna, she turned back to Lou. "I should probably get her home."

"Can we make a pit stop first?" Lou asked Alice, who had driven them all there.

The three ended up a short drive away from Arlington Heights, where Lou and Alice's parents resided. It was a small neighborhood, close to the city. They pulled into the driveway of a small Craftsman that was showing its age. As soon as Alice pulled in the driveway, Lou hopped out and went to fetch Benji from the backseat who was next to Anna. They'd left Caspian at Alice's parents for the evening.

"Where are we?" Anna asked curiously, when Lou had opened the door beside her and retrieved the dog. Benji hopped out of the car just as Alice came around to help her from the car.

"At my friend's house," Lou replied, once they'd all made it to the front of the car. Benji was strapped to a leash. "His name is Walter, but I call him Walty. You should call him Walty."

"Walty's a funny name," Anna replied, as they started up the walkway to the front of the house. When they reached the porch, Lou rang the doorbell a few times and the three waited patiently. An older woman with a head full of curly gray hair answered. The minute she laid eyes on Lou, a smile broke across her face.

"Lou!" The woman said, surprised. "We weren't expecting company."

"Hi Betty," Lou returned the smile. "This is Alice and her daughter Anna. We brought a surprise for Walty. Is he here?"

Walter turned the corner just as Lou had asked of his where-abouts, everybody standing in the doorway as he arrived. "What are you doin' here kid?" He noticed Alice and smiled. "Well hello again, Alice."

"Hi, Walter," Alice said, and watched as Walter's eyes diverted to her daughter. "This is Anna, my daughter."

"Hi, Walty!" Anna exclaimed, without a moment's hesitation. Walter's gaze shot to Lou who was laughing so loudly that it was likely the neighbors could hear her.

"I've got a present for you," Lou finally managed to catch her breath, and looked down at Benji, who was sitting obediently at her feet.

Walter's eyes fell to the dog. He had a strange look on his face, studying him over. Before he was able to get a word in edgewise, Betty spoke for him. "Oh, look Walter, it's a dog! Oh hello, puppy." Betty leaned over to scratch him on the head. "You're so handsome."

"You brought me a dog? What are you doin' to me kid?" Walter eyed Lou, who couldn't contain herself and laughed again.

"He deserves a good home," Lou explained, handing the leash over to Betty. "I couldn't stand leaving him in the shelter any longer."

"So, you brought him to me?" Walter shook his head, but Alice watched his eyes soften when he looked down at the shaggy mutt. He leaned forward, reaching out his hand to let the dog sniff it. Benji licked at his fingers, and Alice watched Walter smile, pleased.

"Dogs are good friends," Anna exclaimed. "I have a dog too."

"You do, do ya?" Walter said, eyeing Anna.

"His name's Caspian," Anna explained, her attention turned toward Walter's voice. "Lou trained him."

"Ah, I know all about Caspian," a smile broke across Walter's face, and he winked at Lou, who was still smiling too. "Well I suppose I should let you in then, mutt?"

"His name is Benji," Lou explained, as she handed him off the leash. "I have some food and supplies in the car for you."

"You wanna stay for dinner?" Walter asked, once he had a hold of the dog.

"I made tuna casserole," Betty added.

"I love casserole!" Anna exclaimed. Lou and Alice hadn't anticipated staying, but after Anna's enthusiasm, Alice couldn't help herself and the three disappeared inside.

Chapter Thirteen

A light early morning breeze hung a very mild chill in the air. The sweet surrendering scent of the morning dew mixed with the overwhelming Douglas-firs that towered above them. Sticks and leaves and brush littered the forest floor, some of them having turned a brittle brown, and there was a sound like dried cereal being crunched underfoot. The dark shadows of the voluminous trees and the surrounding bushes had become the backbone of the forest, standing as passive protectors of a peaceful place. The sun rose in a hurry, blooming into the pale sky with a warm mellow glow.

The shores of Sturgeon Lake were visible through the tree line to Lou and Alice's left. In front of them, Anna walked with Caspian at her side. The dog was enjoying the morning sunshine and the ability to smell the earth around him in peace. Lou and Alice had been lost in conversation as they walked, admiring the scenery of Sauvie Island that morning. It was shaping up to be a beautiful day.

"You *so* had help with that exam," Alice teased her, reminiscing on a final exam they'd taken in an early college class together. "I studied for weeks for it and somehow you barely opened a book and got a better grade."

"I have a photographic memory," Lou said, a smirk stretched across her face. Alice gave her a playful shove and Lou tripped a few paces forward. She gave a quick glance over to Caspian and Anna. This was the first time outside of class that they'd gone together for a walk. Though it was quiet out on the island this morning, she was still careful that the dog was well-behaved. So far, there hadn't been a problem.

There was a brush against Lou's fingers. When she looked down, Alice's hand had lingered near her own for a few brief seconds. It had been that way all morning on their walk. Lou was finding it hard to tell what was going through Alice's mind. If she was starting to want the same things Lou did. Where there had once been a crippling fear of hurting her, there was a newfound confidence now. Unlike anything she'd felt for anyone outside of Alice.

They wound their way down the path toward the shore of the lake. When Lou felt Alice brush her fingers against hers again, she moved her hand swiftly, wrapping them together in one single motion. Their fingers locked together, and Lou held a firm grip on her. The two glanced at one another, and Lou couldn't help but smile.

It felt good like this. She'd needed it for so long and hadn't realized it.

Caspian led them down to the shoreline, whilst Lou made a careful attempt to keep them all away from the water. Once they'd found a picnic table, Alice walked Anna up to it and the three sat down. From her backpack, which Lou had been surprised to find was another Burton, she pulled out lunches for the three of them, and a snack for the dog. Caspian sat on the ground, watching the water with attentive eyes.

While Anna finished her lunch, Lou took a stroll down to the shoreline. She searched along the ground for a good rock. A smooth one that would work. Once she found what she was looking for, she held it in her hand for a minute, admiring its weight and the way it sat in her palm. When she looked back, Alice was watching her curiously. Lou stared back out at the water just for a moment before she sent the rock spinning. It skipped once, twice, three times before it sank underwater.

After tossing another rock, Lou found Alice and Anna had landed beside her, Caspian at their side. "You still throw rocks?" Alice asked, and Lou inclined her head in agreement. The idea seemed to make Alice happy, as a smile crept across her face.

"What's throwing rocks?" Anna asked curiously.

Lou bent down beside her, getting eye level with her. When she spoke, Anna turned her attention toward her. "You toss a rock and make it skip across the water." Lou took a hold of the little girl's hand. With a soft touch, she imitated the rock bouncing along the water on her arm. "Like that, but across the water."

"I want to try," Anna said, without reserve. Lou looked up at Alice, who shrugged.

"Okay, let's give it a shot," Lou agreed. She searched the ground for a small flat rock for Anna to try and throw. Once she had, Lou put it in Anna's hand and wrapped her own around it. "I'm going to help you the first time and then you can try on your own. Okay? Just let go when I get to three." Anna nodded, and Lou turned her a little so she was facing out in the direction of the water. "Here we go. One, Two, Three—" Lou helped her toss the rock out into the water. Surprisingly, it skipped on the first try, sinking down after the second skip.

Behind them, Alice let out a clap of enthusiasm. Lou looked over her shoulder and smiled at her. "Good job, Anna. It skipped. You want to try on your own now? Do you remember how I moved your wrist?" Anna nodded, and Lou fetched her another rock to throw, placing it in her hand ready to throw in the right direction. "Okay. On the count of three. One, two, three—"

The rock whizzed out of the girl's hand and out into the water. It skipped not once, twice, but three times before sinking. Lou stared in awe. She was a natural. "That was amazing Anna. It skipped three times. That's as good as I can skip most of the time."

Anna smiled broadly. "Can I do it again?"

———

Strands of vivid red locks caught the early evening breeze along the Columbia River. The sun's warm light was just starting to disappear over the rooftops of the line of river-front properties. The azure blue waters matched Lou's eyes, which were scanning the surroundings.

Hovering in front of them was a tall white clay brick building, the hues varying from snow white to alabaster. It had a roughness that reminded Lou of rocks on the beach. She stared up at it for a moment, the large weathered sign reading "Oaks Park." Across from her, Alice stood with her eyes closed, hand clasped in Lou's.

"Can I open them yet?" Alice asked. She was dressed in a nice light pink cotton blouse and a pair of jeans, at Lou's insistence. Lou had worn one of her old Death Cab for Cutie T-shirts and a pair of jeans, too. Alice had kept her eyes closed for nearly a half hour now, since they'd left the neighborhood. Lou knew if she started seeing familiar roads, Alice would have known exactly where they were going.

"Okay, open," Lou said, waiting in anticipation as Alice's eyes fluttered open. The streetlamps illuminated the front of the building, along with the remaining sunlight streaking through the sky. Alice gasped in surprise, clapping her hands together. The smile on her face seemed to indicate that she was pleased with where she was. "I told you that you'd like it."

"I can't believe it's still here," Alice said, her voice in disbelief. Her eyes scanned over the length of the building and watched some of the crowd that was already headed inside.

"They've tried to close it a couple of times since you left, but it's hung on." Lou replied, tugging at her hand. Ever since their trip to Sauvie Island, Lou hadn't wanted to let go of her and had used every excuse to hold her again. "Come on."

The roller-skating rink hadn't changed much since Alice and Lou's first date in high school, when they'd nervously held hands in public, and Lou had stolen a kiss from her near the red lockers. They were still there, on the far side of the room as they entered, and Lou could even make out the fluorescent light they'd stood under as she'd whispered how much she'd wanted to kiss her the whole evening. Alice had surprised her, pressing their lips together in one tender moment. Lou hadn't breathed or blinked the entire few seconds they'd been together, fearing if she did, she'd ruin it. But it had been perfect, in every sense of the word.

It was years ago now, but it had felt like yesterday standing in the doorway. When Lou looked at Alice, she was smiling. "Are we going to rent some skates or not?" Lou returned the smile and the pair headed inside, their hands still clasped together. In fact, neither of them let go until they were handed their skates and had to put them on. "I don't remember how to skate, do you?" Alice said, looking nervous. "I'm going to make a fool out of myself."

"We'll make fools of ourselves together," Lou reassured her, after finishing tying the laces on her skates. She got to her feet, wobbling as she held on to the railing that lined the perimeter of the wooden skating rink. The speakers were blasting out *Livin' on a Prayer* by Bon Jovi. The adult skating night always played 80s music, which Alice had always loved in college. A few seconds after Lou had stood, Alice came up to join her, trying to maintain her balance.

"You ready?" she asked, and Lou nodded. Alice took off carefully skating out onto the floor, taking her time. Unlike Lou, she seemed to have a much better handle on things. Lou quivered the entire time, trying to stay steady, and hugged the railing once she'd made it onto the floor. Alice laughed, skating along beside her, finding a groove almost instantly. "Loosen up a little bit."

"Easier said than done," Lou replied, feeling her head spinning from nerves. She could already feel her anxiety causing pinpricks of pain in her chest.

"Breathe, Lou," Alice said softly, reaching down to put their hands together again. The minute they'd found one another, Lou managed to catch her breath. She let air roll in through her mouth and out her nose, in calm, gentle waves. Once she'd gathered her wits, they started off around the rink. Alice on the left while Lou stayed near the railing and tried to get the hang of what she was doing. "There you go. Not so bad, right?"

"I'm glad you're here," Lou said, turning her attention to Alice.

"Me too," Alice smiled at her, and Lou found herself lost in the part between the brown and the green and the blue of her eyes, stuck somewhere in the middle of it all. Alice's soft voice brought her back to reality. "You ready to try and leave the wall?"

Lou took a deep breath and rolled forward, releasing herself from the railing. The pair moved to the middle of the room. Not once did Alice let her go, as the pair moved slowly across the room. Once Lou let go and relaxed, it felt like she was flying on the floor, in slow graceful motions. The world blurred around her. There was nothing in the room except her and Alice together. Again. Like they had been all those years ago. It was like nothing had ever changed.

On the speakers above, Bon Jovi faded and another song began to play. A slow strumming of guitars and familiar chords that Lou hadn't heard in ages. The minute she'd heard it, she recognized it, and turned her attention to Alice. There was a bright smile across her face as she turned her attention to where the music was coming from. *Time After Time* played and Cyndi Lauper's innocent and sweet child-like voice filled the entirety of the building.

Memories of Senior Prom flashed through Lou's mind, with Alice's blonde head laying on her shoulder as they swayed to this very song. It had taken them so long to feel comfortable together in public, especially in high school. When they went to prom, they hadn't cared. Lou could remember Alice singing along to the song softly in her ear as they swayed together.

Alice was singing along again, absorbed in the world around her, and Lou watched her transfixed. Realizing how much the lyrics rang as true as they had fourteen years ago as they did in this very moment. The reality of loving someone unconditionally, even when they were out of time with one another. People changing together and apart, but choosing each other over and over again. Lou realized how much she still loved Alice, even after all these years. How easy and simple she was. How natural it felt.

Time spun around them, but Lou felt encapsulated in that moment as Cyndi's voice rang out above them. The glittering disco lighting refracted off of Alice's golden hair and multi-colored lights sparkled in her mesmerizing eyes. Her eyes had closed briefly, enjoying the feeling of flying across the hardwood skating rink, and Lou wondered what she was thinking in that moment. If she felt as free and alive as Lou had felt, after all these years.

Lou stopped and spun her, watching as she turned and her eyes fluttered open. Their hands came together first, as they paused on the side of the rink, standing still under the twinkling lights above. Those familiar red lockers were behind her when Lou looked up. Alice was still smiling, singing along to the chorus, and it felt as if she was singing it to her. If she was lost, she would find her. If she fell, she would catch her.

Alice was the only person in the world Lou had ever wanted to catch her.

Their lips brushed together, in one singular movement. Not innocently, like a tease, but hot, fiery, passionate and demanding. Lou thought to pull away before she lost herself, but she couldn't seem to. Her senses were seduced, and she could no longer think straight. "Lou," Alice whispered, prolonging each letter like she was savoring them. Lou smiled, her heart fluttering at Alice's voice, as she clasped her hands on either side of Alice's face. Never before had Lou's name felt so wonderful, she thought, as she leaned in for another kiss.

They kissed, and the world fell away. It was slow and soft this time, comforting in ways the world would never be. Lou's hand rested beneath Alice's ear, her thumb caressing her cheek as their breaths mingled. Alice's fingers ran down the length of Lou's spine, pulling her closer until there was no space left between them, and she could feel the beating of her heart against her chest.

Lou wanted this. For the rest of her life she wanted this. She needed it. More than she'd ever needed anything. And as much as she wanted it, it terrified her even more.

Chapter Fourteen

Flecks of golden sunlight spread across the concrete floor of the training facility building in Troutdale. It was proving to be a beautiful day outside, and Alice had wished somewhat that they had gone outside. But then her attention focused back on her daughter.

"Go to the door, Caspian," Anna said. She was holding on to the white plastic handle on the dog's halter, her body facing straight ahead. Alice watched nervously as the dog moved slowly to the right and headed off toward the front door of the room. Meanwhile, Lou followed behind a few steps, keeping watch of what was happening.

Lou being with her daughter made Alice's mind ease. She watched the way Lou paid careful attention to every move Anna and Caspian made, ready to jump in when necessary. Meanwhile, Alice wondered what was going on in her mind. They hadn't spoken much since their outing to the skating rink, even though it had been nearly the only thing on Alice's mind for days.

Anna made it to the door and she reached out to find the handle. Even from the distance she was at, Alice could see her daughter smiling. Lou turned to look over her shoulder at Alice, and gave her a thumbs up. Alice laughed clapping her hands together pleased. "Okay, keep going Anna. Ask Caspian to take you somewhere else."

"Go to the other side of the room, Caspian," Anna instructed him.

Lou made her way back to Alice, and Alice's stomach tied in knots with worry of Anna being on her own this time. When Lou reached her, she wrapped a reassuring hand around Alice's shoulder. "Don't worry, they've got this. I promise." The touch of Lou's hand washed away every fear that was racing through Alice's mind. The touch bringing back memories of a few days prior, when Lou had kissed her at the roller-skating rink. How familiar it had been, and how much she'd missed the taste of her mouth. The kindness of her lips. When she thought about it, she could remember almost every little detail perfectly including the warmth and sweetness that she'd drunk from her lips like a fine wine.

Alice's attention fell back on her daughter again as she felt along the wall and then reached in her pockets for treats. "Good doggie!" Anna said, sticking out her hand. Caspian took them happily. "Go to Mama, Caspian!"

There was a nudge at Alice's side. When she looked at Lou, she was speaking to Anna. "You need to call him now so he knows you're the cue."

"Here, Caspian," Alice said, waving her arms. The dog's ears twitched and his head turned toward Alice's voice.

"To Mama," Anna repeated. With his head held high, Caspian made his way back across the room to join them. Meanwhile, Lou's hand hadn't left Alice's shoulder. The minute the dog reached them, Alice let out a long sigh of relief. "Did he make it?" Anna asked.

"He made it," Alice said, placing a hand on her daughter's head, as Anna rewarded the dog for doing what she'd asked. When Alice looked back up at Lou, she could tell that she'd gotten substantially more nervous than she'd been acting earlier. Class was about to end, and Alice knew exactly why she was acting the way she was. "You're going to be alright, you know. They don't bite."

"Your mother never really liked me much," Lou argued, walking over a few steps to hang a leash on a hook on the wall. She came back to gather up toys from the floor and Alice helped her put them in a bin. "I imagine it's even worse now after everything that's happened."

Alice frowned, and nudged Lou in the side. "My mother loves you." She reached out to grasp Lou's hand in her own, before she'd even thought about it. It felt nice to touch her again. She squeezed softly and smiled again. "She was the one that offered in the first place. Just come over, you'll see. Everything will be fine."

The two made their way back to Anna, who was loving on Caspian and doing "high fives." Caspian was getting so comfortable with her now, it made Alice's heart warm every time they were together. Luckily they'd have the next few days together again. "You ready to go, sweetheart?" Alice asked, and Anna nodded. She got to her feet with the help of the dog. "You don't mind if Lou comes with us to eat dinner at grandma and grandpas, do you?"

"Lou's coming?" Anna's voice raised a half-octave in excitement.

"I'm coming," Lou said, giving Alice another hesitant look, but her lips were smiling.

———

"Quit fidgeting," Alice was busy situating stray pieces of garnet red hair around the side of Lou's face, tucking it behind her ear. Once she'd finished, her hands lingered against Lou's cheek, the tips of Alice's fingers running against her skin. Lou leaned into it and they stayed together for a moment, as if time had stopped still.

"Are we at grandmas?" Anna asked, tugging on Alice's shirt. Caspian sat patiently beside her, wagging his tail. Anna had a grip on his halter. Alice looked down at her daughter, breaking her focus on Lou. She placed a hand on top of her head, and turned her to face the front door, letting them all inside the foyer.

Right inside, Alice was surprised to find her father waiting. Once Alice and her daughter had made it into the room, Lou followed. James' eyes were glued on her. Alice held her breath, wondering what he was going to do. He immediately walked over, stretching out his hand. "It's good to see you, Lou." There was a smile plastered across his face, which Lou returned.

"You too," she replied, before James brought her into a hug.

Through the hallway, Alice could smell the distinct smell of fresh pasta and tomato sauce. Her mother must have been making spaghetti, which had always been a favorite of Lou's when they'd been dating. Alice's heart grew warm at the idea her mother had gone to the trouble of preparing something Lou had once loved so much.

"Lily's just down the hall," James said, nodding in the direction of the kitchen. "Granddaughter, how about we go get washed up for dinner?" Alice's father took hold of Anna's hand while she held the other around Caspian's halter. The three made their way down another hall, with Alice and Lou watching them until they disappeared around a corner.

"You ready?" Alice nudged Lou and then reached for her hand. She wrapped their fingers together and offered a gentle squeeze. Lou's shoulders relaxed and Alice led her down a hallway toward the kitchen. As soon as they'd rounded the corner into the kitchen, Alice released Lou's hand. At the island, her mother was working cutting up mushrooms. The minute they'd entered, Lily turned on a heel to face them. A smile spread across her face. "Oh, Lou," Lily said, walking straight over to meet her. They embraced, without having to say another word to each other. Her mother seemed genuinely happy to see Lou.

"It's nice to see you, Lily," Lou said, once they'd separated. Lily nodded in agreement. "It's been a long time."

Lily smiled, lost in Lou for a moment. Finally she looked over at the sink. "Go wash your hands and then help me with these vegetables. I want to hear all about what you've been up to."

While Lou worked with Lily, wrapped up in conversation, Alice helped her father set the table. When Lou and Lily had finished up cooking the meal, and were bringing it over the table, Anna was talking to James. "Here you go, Anna," Lou said, setting a plate down in front of her. Anna's head turned in the direction of Lou's voice, and turned upward.

"Lou?" Anna asked, as Alice watched as Lou set down Lily's plate on the opposite side of her blonde headed daughter. "Grandpa made you a spot next to me."

"He did, did he?" Lou replied. Alice smiled as the redhead sat in the seat that her daughter had been referring to. "Well that was awfully nice of him."

"I asked him to," Anna said matter-of-factly. Lou's eyes moved in the direction of Alice, and when their gazes met, they both broke into a smile nearly simultaneously. Alice looked back toward her daughter and Lou turned her focus back. "Do you want to know something interesting about sea turtles?"

Alice brought Lou's plate and sat it in front of her. Lou mouthed a gracious 'thank you,' just before she replied. "What about sea turtles?" There was a warmth radiating through Alice, one that swelled from her heart outward in every direction.

"Did you know the largest sea turtle weighs two thousand pounds?" Anna asked. Lou, meanwhile, had gotten the napkin that had been placed by Anna's plate by her grandmother, and placed it in Anna's lap. "That's like—a lot of pounds."

Lou laughed, just as Alice sat down beside her. Instinctively, Alice reached out to grasp Lou's hand in her own, underneath the table. She felt the warmth of her fingers as they intertwined, and instantly felt at peace. When Alice glanced at her parents, both were watching Lou and Alice while they served their food. "That is a lot of pounds," Lou agreed.

"Did—did you know too that they can stay underwater for five hours?" Anna piped up again. "I can't stay underwater that long, can I Mama?"

"Not quite that long," Alice said, squeezing Lou's hand softly before she let go to serve the pasta. She put some of the spaghetti on Lou's plate, before serving herself. Meanwhile, Lily was trying to gather Anna's attention to the food on her plate.

"Alice says you live in Adam's place?" James asked, taking a bite of pasta. Alice wondered how Lou would react to this bit of information, but she seemed to take it in her stride.

"I do," she replied, smiling. "Stephen didn't want it after he passed away, so I just decided to stay there."

"Had I known you were right down the street, we'd have invited you over," Lily said matter-of-factly. Alice figured her mother was being polite, but it was a nice gesture regardless. "You should come over more often now."

"I'll make a point to," Lou smiled at her, twirling some pasta around her fork.

"We've been trying to get the kiddo to move back home," James said, nudging Alice. Alice rolled her eyes. Trying had been an understatement. It was a constant conversation ever since she'd divorced Jeremy. Truthfully, if it hadn't been for him, she probably would have come. It was lonely in Seattle. Her father knew why she couldn't leave, and he didn't press it further, just smiled at her.

"I do miss Portland," Alice agreed, finishing up the last bite of food on her plate. "You want to help me wash dishes?" Alice looked at Lou, who quickly rose to her feet. The two of them collected the plates, while Lily, James and Anna made their way over to the couch in the living room. A Disney movie was playing on TV, which Anna loved to listen to.

Lou started the water in the sink. She'd always loved to wash dishes by hand, a trait that seemed after all the years that had passed, she still practiced. She watched as Lou scrubbed off a plate in the sink, rubbing it clean with a sponge. Once she'd finished, Lou handed it to Alice, who was still staring at her. "You gonna dry?"

Alice shook her head free of lingering thoughts and nodded. She fetched a dish towel and took the plate from Lou. Together they washed some of the plates in silence, a very familiar rhythm between them. Alice couldn't help but admire Lou as she worked. She was busy focused intently on a pot, scrubbing off spaghetti sauce. Memories of when they used to do this together when they'd been dating came racing back.

A quick glance in the living room let Alice know that her parents and daughter were still distracted with the television. Meanwhile, Alice stepped behind Lou, brushing her red hair around one shoulder as she continued to work. Her hands wrapped around

Lou's waist, mouth falling onto the crook of her neck. Breathing in her familiar scent that still smelled of herbs, particularly lavender this time around. Alice breathed deeply, taking as much of it in as she could. Her lips made a trail from Lou's neck up to her earlobe. She could feel Lou's breath quickening as she finished the pot and placed it on the counter to dry.

Lou's hand gripped hold of Alice's that was lingering at the hem of her shirt, wanting desperately to touch the soft skin that lay underneath. The thoughts that were racing through her were causing a burning through her body, straight between her legs. Alice pushed the two of them together tightly, hoping to stop the now persistent throbbing.

Lou broke away from her in one fluid motion and made her way around the island. Alice watched her, unsure of what to think. "I'm going to have to head out for the evening," Lou announced to James and Lily, and Alice's daughter. "Thanks for dinner. It was nice to see you both." Lily got up from her seat to walk over and wrap her arms around Lou's neck. Lou hugged her back briefly.

"Come visit again soon?" Lily asked, and Lou nodded.

"Bye, Lou!" Anna called out, as Lou turned her attention back to Alice. Alice could have sworn she was looking straight at her lips in such a devouring way that it caused a shiver to rip through her.

"Bye, Anna," Lou replied, making haste out of the kitchen and down the hall.

"I'm going to walk her out," Alice announced, following only steps behind Lou as she made her way to the front door. Lou didn't stop until she'd made it outside. The screen door had barely snapped closed behind Alice, when Lou spun around, pulling Alice to the side of the door frame and up against the outer wall of the house, pinning her.

Lou's steady gaze bore into Alice in silent expectation, traveling over her face and searching for her eyes. She was as eager and erratic as a summer storm. Alice watched as Lou dipped closer, eyes popping with a sheen of purpose. She stood frozen as her senses leapt to life, knees weakened by the quivering of her limbs. Lou's mouth covered hers, hungrily, her tongue tracing the fullness of her lips. The kiss was urgent and exploratory, and Alice's mind unwound at the warmth and ravishment of it.

Alice couldn't discern where the heat was coming from between them. Her heart pounded in an erratic rhythm as Lou buried her face in Alice's neck, breathing kisses there. Lou's head fit perfectly in the hollow between her shoulder and neck. Alice could feel her uneven breathing against her skin, as she held her close. Alice imagined what she'd be like to touch again, curling into the curve of her body. Skin to skin. A soft moan escaped her as Lou's mouth grazed her earlobe. "Come away with me this weekend," Lou whispered, before kissing the shell of her ear.

It was all Alice wanted, to be alone with Lou. The entire weekend. Nothing stopping them. But her mind jolted back to her daughter, who was just inside. "I can't leave Anna."

Lou pulled away from her, but her hands still sat on either side of Alice's body, pinning her to the wall. They stared at one another and Alice thought Lou's piercing blue eyes would burn a hole straight through her. "Then come with me tomorrow. We'll go over to the coast. I'll make it worth your while."

Alice smiled at her, pondering her suggestion for just a moment, and then looked deeply into her eyes. "Only if you kiss me again," she whispered in reply. Lou wasted no time, pressing her open lips to Alice's. There was a dreamy intimacy to their kisses now, and Alice savored every second until she pulled away. Lou released her, heading down the steps without another word, and Alice watched, with weakened legs, as she disappeared into the night.

Chapter Fifteen

The world danced around outside as Lou joined the pedestrian packed streets of downtown Astoria that were now fluttering with life. Colorful food trucks lined the streets, while a steady flow of traffic passed the storefronts along the Columbia River. A flyer for a local Oregon band hung on the large picture window that adorned the front of a thrift shop. Lou watched the scene inside, as if it were unfolding in a movie. The blue wall reminded Lou of a stormy sea, a deep blue mixed with gray. A familiar blonde, with short cropped hair, was perusing through the aisles, pausing on different things as she went. At the moment, her fingers were lightly touching the edges of an antique lantern that hung from the ceiling.

Lou admired the delicateness about the way she moved and appreciated each thing she touched. The lightness in her eyes. She looked content, without a care in the world. It was the way Lou loved seeing her most, and what she had missed the most. When Alice turned to look over her shoulder and locked eyes with Lou, she waved her inside. Lou's thoughts evaporated and she walked in to join her.

"Look at this," Alice extended her hand and Lou took it without reservation. The two weaved their way through the collection of knickknacks until they fell upon an old dusty painting that had been tucked away in a corner. Alice peeled away the things that were sitting around it to show Lou. "What do you think?"

Lou couldn't help but smile. The dog in the painting looked strikingly similar to Caspian, chasing after something in a field. His legs were in mid-trot, with beautiful wildflowers surrounding him. Lou studied it for a long while, the smile on her face unwavering. "I think we should buy it," Alice announced. The two looked down at the price tag at the same time and Lou watched Alice's facial expression drop. "Holy crap." She was staring at the fifty dollar price tag.

"I wouldn't have any place to put it," Lou argued, trying to make her feel better.

Alice frowned, weaving her way through the store, leaving Lou where she was. A minute later she returned with a woman with graying brown hair. "We were wondering if we could get this for twenty dollars."

"I won't go any lower than thirty," the woman replied, giving Alice a stubborn look.

Lou knew Alice would never back down from a good bartering. It wasn't her first rodeo thrift store shopping. "Not even twenty five?" Alice gave her a friendly smile.

The woman pondered for a moment. "Fine, twenty five dollars." Alice fished through her pockets for the money and handed it over to her, looking rather satisfied. Once she'd gotten the painting, the two headed out of the shop. When they rounded onto the sidewalk, Alice handed the painting to Lou. "Here you go. Something to remember Caspian by."

Lou wanted to argue, but the words had stung her worse than she'd anticipated. *Something to remember Caspian by.* Soon Caspian would no longer be in her life, and what made it all the worse was it was true of Alice too. Before long, she'd be back in Seattle with Anna and her dog companion of two years. This thing that was growing between them was all just temporary.

But she'd make it last as long as she could.

A short drive from Astoria, they ended up on the coastline of Washington state, in Long Beach. During college, it was a popular weekend get-away for the pair. Lou hadn't been to the Washington coast in years, preferring not to rehash old memories. But today had felt as good a time to go as any. Surprisingly the old beachside restaurant was still open. The Pickled Prawn was a popular dive amongst the locals. Lou and Alice had discovered it on a whim while walking along the beach many years ago.

"They still have the mushroom pizza!" Alice exclaimed when she'd had the menu in her hand. She sighed softly. "Are we going to get the mushroom pizza?"

Lou smiled at her and nodded, just as the waitress had come up to the table. "I'll have a sweet tea," Lou said. "And we'll split the mushroom pizza."

"Sweet tea for me too," Alice agreed. "With a slice of lemon."

The waitress took their menus and wandered off, leaving the two alone. From their seat outside, Lou could make out the beach a small distance away. It wasn't the perfect view, but it was as pretty of a view as she'd had in a long time. She watched the waves roll in for a few minutes, before she felt Alice's hand wrap around her own at the table.

"Where are you at?" Alice asked. Lou hadn't even noticed that their drinks had been dropped off at the table.

"Just thinking," Lou replied, looking at her. "It's been a long time since I've been out here. I'm surprised how little it's changed."

"Yeah, I know," Alice agreed, squeezing her hand and smiling. "Nice to be back, huh?"

"It really is," Lou agreed. "And with you." Alice's cheeks grew rosy, but she looked pleased nevertheless, and she didn't let go of her hand. Not until the pizza had come a few short minutes later. They ate together, enjoying the scenery and laughing about old times together. The entire night felt effortless.

As they were finishing off their final slices, a band started to play across the patio outside. A jazz band that Lou was unfamiliar with, but that was reminiscent of the kind of music that used to play there all those years ago. "Oh, they're playing music," Alice sighed, looking at Lou. Before she could say anything else, Lou shook her head, knowing what was going to come out of her mouth. "Oh come on, dance with me just this once. You never did before."

It was the right thing to say, and a pang of guilt rushed through Lou at her words. Every time they'd come here when they'd been dating, Lou had made excuses why she wouldn't dance with her. Alice had even danced on her own sometimes, while Lou watched. But they'd never danced together, outside of prom. Lou blamed it mostly on her anxiety.

Lou bit her lip, pondering for a half second. Already, there were a handful of couples that had gotten up to dance together. Finally, Lou got up from her seat and extended a hand. "Come on then."

"Are you serious?" Alice laughed, clapping her hands together before she took Lou's. "After all this time, Lou Pearson is finally dancing with me." Lou rolled her eyes, leading Alice up to the front near the band, where there was an empty area of space to move. They slid in alongside an older couple who swayed quietly to the music. Alice sighed happily, wrapping her arms around Lou's neck. They swayed back and forth, Alice smiling the entire time. "Thank you," she mouthed.

"Thank you," Lou replied back, leaning in to kiss her swiftly on the mouth. Alice laid her head on Lou's shoulder, getting lost in the music. Meanwhile, Lou took in the ambiance of the room around them, holding Alice close to her as they swayed to the slower jazz song. Smelling the mix of the salty air and the way Alice's hair smelled like honey and wildflowers as she held her in her arms. The way her hair tickled against Lou's cheek. The soft sounds of her sighs and breathing as they danced.

Lou could have held onto that moment forever. She wanted to, desperately. It had been something she'd wanted since she'd lost it all those years ago.

How lucky she was to be alive in that moment, to be here. To feel free.

The sun had disappeared into the ocean by the time they'd left for the evening. It had grown ominously cloudy, and a little chillier than Lou had expected. She let Alice use her jacket as they made their way back to her yellow Volkswagen. Almost as soon as they'd hopped inside, it started to pour outside.

"We always get rained on," Alice laughed.

"Welcome to the Pacific Northwest," Lou replied, reaching over to take Alice's hand. "Did you have a good time?"

"It was wonderful but I'm still having a good time," Alice said, smiling at her. She leaned over to kiss Lou softly on the cheek. "But you'd better get me back home, I'm going to miss my curfew." It was a joke, but the last thing Lou wanted was to take her home. She tightened her grip on Alice's hand slightly and leaned in, pressing her lips to Alice's, caressing her mouth more than kissing it. She drank in the sweetness of Alice's lips, and forced her lips open with a thrusting tongue. Alice kissed her back devouringly, wrapping her hand around Lou's cheek.

Lou's senses short-circuited, and her consciousness seemed to ebb and then flow more distinctly than ever. She breathed Alice in, every piece of her, as her hands wrapped into the shirt wisps of blonde hair, pulling her closer.

A blaze of lightning tore through the night sky, followed by a booming crack of thunder. The noise sent the pair both jumping almost instantly, breaking their heated kisses. Lou sat back against the seat, panting softly and laughing. "You better get me home, Ms. Pearson," Alice clicked her tongue, smiling.

"I probably should," Lou agreed, putting the keys into the ignition. She twisted and the car sputtered. As soon as it did, Lou's heart sunk. She turned it again, and the car sputtered again, not starting. "Shit," Lou muttered under her breath, twisting the key for a third time, to no avail.

"It won't start?" Alice asked, and Lou sighed. "It does this sometimes when the rain gets in the engine. It's normally fine in a couple of hours once it dries out." The two sat in the car in silence, watching the rain pour outside in the darkness, lightning tearing through the sky. Alice looked outside, scanning the surroundings, and Lou watched her thinking quietly to herself for a minute. She pulled out her phone, quickly searching for something. Finally, she turned back to Lou, a smile on her face. "Are you up for a little run in the rain?"

Running in the rain did not sound like a fun time to Lou, and she wasn't quite sure what Alice had in mind. "Where to?" Lou asked curiously. "We're better off waiting here for a tow truck."

"It'll take forever this time of night and by morning it should be fine," Alice argued. Lou watched her type a text message on the screen to "Dad," presumably letting her parents know that they were stuck for the evening. "Come on. Just trust me. It's only two blocks." Alice reached out to open the handle on her side of the car. Lou still gave her a questionable look. The idea did not sound enticing in the least. "Oh and try not to get struck by lightning."

Before Lou could stop her, she watched Alice disappear from the car. A second later, Lou followed behind her, booming thunder above them. They scrambled in the rain down the beach front street. Lou somehow managed to find Alice's hand in the darkness, and they ran as fast as their feet could carry them. When they finally turned a corner onto a large lot, Lou realized where she'd taken them.

They'd passed this place a thousand times driving from Portland years ago. It was a tourist trap for the area. Another place that Alice had always wanted to go to, but Lou had always argued with her against. On the neon sign hanging out front were the words "Vacancy".

The vintage trailer motels were one of a kind, Lou hadn't ever seen anything like them. And right now, in the pouring rain, they seemed like the most wonderful thing in the world. Alice darted into the open office, Lou trailing behind her. The pair stood letting pools of water drip off of them for a minute as they gathered their bearings. A scrawny looking man who reminded Lou very much of Walter, stood behind a desk. He watched them as they made their way up, a long line of water falling behind them.

"Sorry about your floor," Alice said, looking embarrassed. The man disappeared for a minute around the corner and when he returned he had two towels. Both Alice and Lou each took one, drying themselves off as best they could. "We were wondering if you had a room available for the night."

While the man and Alice worked on getting a room squared away, Lou wiped up the floor as best she could with the towel. When she finally turned her attention back, Alice was waving a key on a ring in her face. "Guess we get to spend the night together after all," she smiled, somewhat mischievously.

Lou could think of nothing better in that moment. The two left their towels with the manager and headed back out into the rain. It had slowed a little, but everything else had too. They hadn't run this time, walking through the rain without much care. Searching through the lot of vintage silver trailers for their own. It was nestled in the back, under a large oak tree. Lou watched Alice walk up the short set of wooden steps to the door. Once she'd gotten it open and stepped inside, Lou followed in after her.

The place had a very eclectic flair to it. It was decorated in a sixties style, with vintage framed posters on the walls, shaggy carpet rugs on hardwood floors, and a marvelous looking plush red comforter on a queen sized bed in the back. Lou's eyes only briefly scanned their surroundings, instead watching Alice as she approached.

"You're wet," Alice noted, her face only centimeters from Lou's, staring at her with an overwhelming sense of longing. A shudder passed through Lou, the likes of which she'd never felt before.

"So are you," Lou breathed, just as she reclaimed her lips, crushing Alice to her. Lou's fingers fumbled furiously at the pearl white buttons of her blue blouse, ripping it from her body as quickly as she could. Once it fell to the floor in a heap, Alice's fingers worked under Lou's fitted T-shirt, until it fell beside her own.

A blur of fingers and fabric took over, as clothes ripped from their bodies. Lou's mouth throbbed with the intensity of Alice's kisses. When they finally broke away from one another, Alice was completely naked.

Eight years. Sometimes in fleeting memories when she was alone, Lou would try to remember what Alice had looked like. Mostly she'd gotten the image right. The small birthmark on her hip. The way her breasts looked, one just a hair bigger than the other. The flush of her skin when she was naked and aroused. It was the same now, just as she'd imagined it, but so real now. She could smell the scent of her nakedness in that room, breathed it in, in sharp, ragged breaths.

Alice was studying her too, in silence. She reached out and touched Lou's cheek softly with the tips of her fingers, and Lou felt her cheeks color at the heat of her gaze. Alice's finger traced the full length of Lou's lips, and a quiver surged through her veins.

"I've missed you," Alice whispered, in the darkness, and Lou let out a resounding cry of happiness, her heart thundering in her chest. She twisted Alice into her arms, molding their soft curves to the contours of their bodies. Lou could feel Alice's uneven breathing against her, and her body tingled from the contact. Her emotions whirled and skidded.

"I've missed you too," Lou whispered, smothering the words on Alice's lips.

Chapter Sixteen

Lou studied Alice, unhurriedly, one piece at a time, a heart rendering tenderness in her gaze. Alice felt as if her heart could burst, watching those deep blue eyes trace every inch of her. As Lou's slow, seductive stare trickled downward, Alice felt heat grow on her cheeks, and something intense flared through her entrancement. There was a whirlwind of emotions ripping through Alice, all at once. Emotions that made her skin feel as though a thousand little tiny fires were ablaze across it. Emotions that made her thoughts whir and spin like mad. Here she was again, after all these years, in the arms of the only person she'd ever truly loved. Completely vulnerable and helpless to those eyes, shimmering orbs that were capturing the very essence of her being. That knew, even though Alice hadn't said it, to be patient, and soft, and calm.

Lou knew her. Lou had always known her.

They fell together on the plush red comforter, Lou's body smothering Alice's. Encapsulating her with its warmth. Alice sighed as soft lips etched a path from her mouth along her cheekbone and down into her neck. Every warm kiss like a piercing shockwave that rippled through her. She paused at the soft space between the curve that led to her collarbone. A special spot that only Lou had ever known. Her mouth floated above it, and Alice could feel her breathing growing ragged. The prolonged anticipation was almost unbearable. But then those soft pink lips fell onto the heat of her skin, and Alice moaned, happily, feeling the heat between her legs, a dull pulsing thud now, begging for release.

Lou pulled away and a hand seared a path from the curve of Alice's cheek, over her lips, down her throat and onto her collarbone. Gently, she outlined the circle of Alice's breast, and Alice's thoughts spun. Once again, Lou's mouth returned to Alice's collarbone, kissing downward. Alice's heartbeat throbbed against her ear. Lou's hand slid across Alice's silken belly, while her tongue caressed a marble hard nipple. Alice erupted into a soft moan, back arching toward Lou, curling into the curve of her body.

Lou took her time, touching every inch of bare skin, like she was memorizing every piece. The touches were followed by kisses that trailed down to her belly button and then stopped as Lou adjusted herself, her hand snaking seductively down Alice's body. The stroking of Lou's fingers on her pelvic bone sent pleasant jolts through Alice, moving magically lower and lower with each touch. Aroused now, she drew herself closer to Lou, clutching her fingers in the curls of garnet red. Lou's mouth drew upward again to explore the rosy peak of her other breast. Alice moaned softly into the room, unable to contain herself.

Alice gasped when Lou's hands moved even farther down, skimming either side of the inside of her thighs. Taunting her. Instinctively, her body arched in Lou's direction again, which, after Lou removed her mouth from Alice's nipple, brought a smile to her lips. Alice tried desperately to kiss her, to no avail, and instead watched her beautiful blue eyes as they stared down at her. Lou's mouth hung slightly open, in a very concentrated way, as Alice felt her caress between her legs. Her body melted against hers. The world spun and careened on its axis.

Alice moved for Lou again, and their mouths collided together once more, warm and sweet. Alice's uncontrollable outcry of delight erupted into Lou's mouth, unable to disguise her body's reaction. Fingers spread her apart, dipping down to graze her swollen clit.

Alice's hips thrust upward again as Lou found a rhythm to her touches, running circles around her slick middle.

When Alice opened her eyes again, she found Lou's blue eyes watching her intently. As soon as they'd locked on to one another, a finger plunged inside of Alice in a smooth and precise motion, and her world exploded. She writhed beneath her, gasping for air. Crying out Lou's name softly, lips quivering as her mouth fell on Alice's again. Alice's thoughts fragmented, as an electric shock scorched through her body. Her breath came in long surrendering moans as her body clamped onto Lou's fingers, thrusting inside of her.

It was as if a brilliant warm golden light had washed over her and filled her to the brim. Every anxious, nervous piece of her had calmed and every shred of doubt that this had been a hasty decision vanished. This was how it was supposed to be. It made sense. It felt real. Like she'd finally found the missing piece of her that she'd so desperately been searching for. It was here. In this room. With this woman. It was everything she had been missing for so long. And the emotions that came with this sudden realization nearly made Alice cry in overwhelming joy. Instead, a desire to show Lou how much she mattered in that moment consumed her.

Alice felt her body fall back into the sheets. Lou's eyes still hadn't left her, but they'd softened. She pressed their lips together again and Alice sighed. Then, she moved forward, twisting Lou in one swift motion so that they'd switched places against the bedsheets.

It had been eight years since Alice had tasted her. The only woman she'd ever been with. Eight years since she'd smelled the sweet smell between her legs, and she was lustful for it now. Alice planted a surprisingly gentle kiss on Lou's mouth before burying herself in Lou's neck, kissing the pulsing hollow at the base of her throat. She moved farther down, until her lips touched the nipple of Lou's breast with tantalizing possessiveness. With a free hand, she grasped the other with her fingers, twisting and teasing her nipple until it had hardened.

Lou whispered her name in a pleasured moan, which only fueled Alice further. Her kisses trailed hungrily downward, fingers light and painfully teasing. Past her belly button, until they were buried in the hairs on her pelvic bone. Alice's body drifted downward, until she found her mouth barely an inch from the wet lips of Lou's middle. Her fingers traced them, and she watched as Lou's hips bucked and her breath hitched in her throat. When Alice's eyes looked up at her, she was watching intently, having propped herself up on the bed slightly.

Alice's fingers spread her apart, savoring the sight of Lou in her most vulnerable state. The smell of her arousal was tantalizing now. The hungry, pleading look in her eyes imploring Alice to quickly reach her goal. A small smile breached her lips, just as her mouth fell between her splayed fingers, and sucked Lou's twitching clit into her mouth.

A whimpering moan filled the room. Lou fell back onto the bed, hands reaching to hold Alice's head in place. Alice breathed her in, tasting the sweetness of her and enjoying the feeling of Lou's quivering body being pleasured by her touch. Her tongue traced circles, while her fingers found the entrance inside of her.

Two. She'd always liked two. Alice slid them in slowly, as a tormented groan fell from Lou's lips. Lou's hands pushed Alice's mouth deeper in between her legs, while Alice's fingers built a steady rhythm. Lou's breathing went ragged. It didn't take very long before Alice felt the pulsing squeezes around her fingers, clamping tightly. Lou let herself go, crying out into the room, body writhing under Alice's touch.

When Lou finally relaxed, her hands softened against Alice's head. Alice lifted from her, crawling over the top of her until their mouths met, in a series of slow, shivering kisses. Their mouths were warm and sweet together. And nothing else existed in the world.

And it was everything that Alice remembered it to be.

A buzzing of a phone jerked Alice up from the bed. When she reached for it, Jeremy's name was plastered across the screen. Alice squinted, trying to wake herself as best she could. It was early the following morning, the sun just starting to peek through the windows. Lou had stirred beside her, but still hadn't woken. Scrambling, Alice found a pair of robes inside the small bathroom, and wrapped one around her. She walked outside to the front steps of the trailer, sitting down right outside the door.

"Hello?" Alice answered, just before the phone stopped ringing.

"Alice?" Jeremy's voice was a pleasant surprise on the other end of the line. "How are things going?"

They'd talked a few times since Alice had come to Portland, but it had been less than when she'd been in Seattle. Usually they saw each other every week because of Anna. "Everything's good," she replied, squinting as she looked out toward the sunrise. "Is everything okay? It's early."

"I'm on my way to school. We had a project that needed to be finished today, so I'm working on the weekend." Jeremy laughed. "I just thought I'd call and check on you guys."

"Everything's fine," Alice reassured him. She looked back over her shoulder when she heard knocking at the window. Lou was staring down at her. Alice smiled and waved, pointing at her phone. Lou gave her a sexy grin and disappeared.

"Looking forward to getting back home next week?" Jeremy asked.

Was it next week? Time had flown by so fast, she couldn't believe it. The realization hit her like a tsunami. "I guess it is next week," Alice muttered.

"You forgot you were coming home next week?" Jeremy laughed. "You must be having a better time with your parents than I thought."

Alice hesitated. Feeling the emotions that were suddenly hitting her taking over her thoughts. She let out a long sigh into the phone and ran a hand through her hair. Across the way a family of three was coming out of another similar sized trailer. She watched them head out to the parking lot, lost in conversation. "You know, I'm not fine," Alice finally said.

"What's going on?" Jeremy asked, a hint of concern in his voice.

The last few weeks Alice had neglected to tell Jeremy about

running into Lou, and she wasn't quite sure why. Now, however, felt as good a time as any to be honest. "I ran into Lou."

"You ran into Lou?" Jeremy echoed. "Lou Pearson? Your ex-girlfriend?"

"Mm," Alice replied, sinking back against the door of the trailer. She could smell something in the air. Coffee, it seemed like, but she wasn't sure if it was coming from their trailer or not. "She works at the guide dog training facility."

"She works at the training facility?" Jeremy repeated again. It seemed as though he was trying to process the idea. "Lou is one of the trainers?"

"Yep, she's one of the trainers," Alice confirmed. "We've been spending a lot of time together."

"Is that a good thing or a bad thing?" Jeremy asked, and Alice was surprised how open and caring he was about the situation. That had always been Jeremy though, so it shouldn't have come as a surprise.

"Good," Alice replied, smiling at the thought of Lou. "Really good. Except now I'm struggling about leaving. We've kind of reconnected."

"Ah," Jeremy replied. There was a silence on the line and just as Alice was about to ask him if he was still there, he finally cleared his throat.

"I'm coming home though—" Alice reassured him. "Just feeling sad at leaving."

"Can you stay in touch this time?" Jeremy said thoughtfully. "Seattle's only three hours away from Portland. It wouldn't be that bad of a drive. You could do that on the weekends no problem."

Alice hadn't thought of that. They were closer than she thought. The idea put her at ease. Maybe they could make it work somehow this time. Maybe it wasn't impossible. "Thanks, Jeremy."

"See you next week?" Jeremy said.

"See you next week," Alice echoed.

When Alice returned inside the trailer, Lou was watching her from across the room still in bed. She yawned, wiping sleep from her eyes. "Who was that?"

"Jeremy, just calling to check up on things," Alice answered, making her way across the room. She sat down on the edge of the bed, her relaxed mood having grown a little more serious. It seemed as if Lou could sense the tension in her posture and she sat up in bed studying her over for a minute. She didn't need to ask, Alice continued anyway. "Do you think we could make this work? If we tried long distance?"

Lou's face twisted slightly in surprise, looking as if she hadn't been expecting Alice to say that. She pondered on it for a moment, keeping quiet. Finally, a small smile breeched her face. "Do you want to be long distance?"

"I know I don't want this to end," Alice said matter-of-factly. "I know we ended it before and it was the worst decision I ever made."

"I don't want it to end either," Lou agreed. "I just wasn't sure what you wanted."

Their moment was interrupted by the buzz of a cell. This time, it wasn't Alice's but Lou's that was in her jeans pocket. Lou slid off the side of the bed, fishing for it. She studied the number, puzzled. "Wrong number," she muttered, setting the phone back onto the bed.

"We'll make it work," Alice reassured her. "Don't worry."

The cell buzzed again on the bed this time. A voicemail message alert flashed on the screen. Lou stared down at the phone again, finally deciding to pick it up. She punched the button to dial her voice mail and put the phone to her ear. Alice watched her as she sat and listened to what sounded like a woman speaking on the other end. Lou's face dropped, and Alice felt a wave of worry wash over her.

When Lou dropped the phone back onto the bed, she looked as though she was struggling to breathe. "Who was that?" Alice asked, concern laced in her voice.

"It was Betty," Lou said, ashen faced and hardly audible.

"Betty?" Alice tried to make sense of what she was saying. It looked as though Lou was about to pass out, and the way she was looking was frightening her. "Lou, are you okay?"

"Something's happened to Walter," Lou breathed.

Chapter Seventeen

The hospital waiting area had about as much personality inside as it did out. The floor was a slate gray, the walls a pale blue with drywall that showed through like white scars. The cheap prints on the walls were insipid, so lacking in vibrancy that they appeared sun-bleached in the windowless room. Above, the ceiling was made from polystyrene squares laid in a grid-like frame. The lighting was too bright for Lou, her eyes still adjusting after being in a car for two hours as they'd driven back to Portland. It was abrasive, bringing a sharp pain between her eyebrows.

The last time Lou had been in a hospital had been with Stephen and Kelly years ago, when the siblings' father, Adam, had passed away. Lou hated hospitals. All the noise and the constant rush of staff running from room to room stirred her anxiety. This time it was no different. The only reason she was able to stay calm was because of Alice, who had been holding steady onto her hand since they'd entered the building.

"Walter Harris," Lou repeated to the triage nurse. The thoughts in her head were jumbled. Every nerve in her body was on fire. All she wanted was to see Walter. To know he was safe. "I'm here to see Walter Harris."

A loud 'pop' of gum vibrated off the surrounding walls. The unenthused woman with obviously dyed black hair, with her light brown roots showing and glazed over hazel eyes that looked as though they'd lost their zest for life years ago, chewed noisily on her gum. She looked lost in whatever it was she was doing on her computer. "Excuse me—" Lou tried again, but she was interrupted by an abrupt motion of a finger.

"One second," the woman snapped. Alice's face twisted into one of annoyance, but Lou squeezed her hand softly and it seemed to calm her. "Name?"

"Walter Harris," Lou repeated herself, trying to keep her voice calm and collected.

"Relation?" The nurse asked, hazel eyes giving her a once-over.

"I'm his friend—" Lou was starting to feel rather impatient, wishing she could just get behind the automatic doors. She'd ask someone else if she had to. Literally *anyone* at this point would do.

"I'm sorry, we're only letting immediate family back," the nurse said.

This time, Alice was the one that couldn't hold her patience. "We've just driven over two hours from Washington to get here. He's her best friend. I'd appreciate it if you just tell us where he is."

"Lou!" A familiar voice called out from across the room. Standing in the hallway was the familiar short gray haired woman, with the wire framed glasses and glossy red nail polish on her fingers. There was a look on her face that Lou couldn't read. She didn't bother with the triage nurse anymore, instead tugging Alice along in the direction of Betty.

As soon as Lou had made it over to her, Betty engulfed her in an all-consuming hug. A desperate hug that terrified Lou to her very core. Every ounce of dread poured into Lou through that hug. It was dark and brooding, and Lou begged with every fiber of her being for it to never end so she didn't have to hear what was going to come next.

"Would you like to see him?"

The walk down the hallway to Walter's room was a blur of colors and a jarring melody of sounds that were sending Lou's body into fits. It was hard to breathe, hard to think. The only lifeline that she had tethering her to the ground now was the grip Alice had on her hand. Not so tight that it was painful, but firm enough for Lou to know that she wasn't alone.

Betty paused in front of the room and they all came to an abrupt halt. The world stood still in that moment, and Lou held onto it, trying to save those last few seconds before her reality would become shattered completely. When Betty disappeared, Lou continued onward, following her around the corner and into the room.

There was an eerie darkness within, the kind that enveloped Lou when she stepped into the room. It turned her blood cold and sent a shiver down her spine. It was the kind of darkness that crushed the spirit.

There in the half-light was Walter. Sweet, kind Walter, who had been her anchor for eight years. He was now lying across a bundle of glowing white hospital bedsheets and a machine was breathing for him. The last time Lou had seen one, it had been attached to her father. A steady stream of sounds came from the other equipment that was attached to Walt's thin frame, a monitor bleeping as his heartbeat ran across the screen.

At the foot of the bed, Benji laid curled up at Walter's feet, watching with big brown eyes as they all walked into the room.

"It was early this morning," Betty explained as she went to sit beside Walter. Lou followed, somewhat automatically, like her instincts had taken over any semblance of a plan of what to do. Lou found the side of the hospital bed, sitting beside Walter and next to Benji. She'd let go of Alice, who'd now wrapped her hand around Lou's shoulder. There was no breaking away from Walt. All Lou could do was watch him, in sheer disbelief.

Benji's wet nose found Lou's hand that rested on the bed, and she found the strength to pet the dog, even though the gravity of the situation was crushing her to the Earth. Her long dainty fingers scratched through the dogs shaggy fir, and amidst everything, it was a small comfort.

"Was it a stroke?" Alice said quietly behind Lou. Betty confirmed that it was. But he was alive. He was breathing. The monitor beside his bed was showing the rhythmic lines of his heart beating. Lou stared at him, watching the rise and fall of his chest. The softness of his face.

"They've told me he's brain dead," Betty's voice quivered as she delivered the devastating news. Lou felt Alice shift behind her and assumed she must be offering some sort of comfort to the woman. All she could do, however, was pet the dog beside her, while she watched Walt. Unable to move or think. Betty and Alice chatted behind her for what felt like an eternity. When the haze of her thoughts settled a little, Lou turned to look over her head back at Alice and Betty.

"He wanted me to give this to you," Betty said, digging through her purse. She pulled out a piece of folded paper and handed it to Lou. Scribbled in Walter's chicken scratch handwriting was the name Martha Winters, and a telephone number. "She needed a new sponsor," Betty explained. Lou felt a lump forming in her throat and fought every urge to cry.

"Can I have the room for a minute?" Somehow Lou managed to find her voice, though it came out cracked and barely audible. Betty and Alice nodded nearly simultaneously. The woman was about to fetch her dog, when Lou stopped her. "He can stay." It didn't seem like Benji had any intention of moving anyway.

It felt like the minute the door had closed, Lou had been hit by an enormous wave that knocked the wind out of her. Even through the torrent of emotions she was feeling, even with the fear of being alone, somehow Lou still managed to breathe through it. Knowing that Alice Gray was just on the other side of the door waiting for her made it somewhat more bearable.

Even if the pain was crippling, like she was bleeding out. Like her heart was quitting.

"Oh, Walty," Lou breathed, a shaky hand managing to find his wrinkled one. When she touched him, he was still warm. She could still feel the steady rhythm of his breathing, but she had to convince herself it was just an illusion. Walter wasn't breathing on his own anymore. It wasn't really him. Not anymore.

Tears streamed down Lou's face then, in silent waves. She sucked in air, keeping herself steady. Calm. Despite the crushing sadness that was threatening to overwhelm her. Lou leaned closer, placing her head against his. She could feel Benji shifting his position behind her, but the dog didn't leave. Lou breathed in Walter's scent. Trying to remember every small detail about him. The faintness of the cigars he loved. That lemon fresh smell he always had because of his hair. She took it all in, gasping as she took deep breaths of air. Savoring every second she could.

"*God,*" Lou whispered into the darkness. *"Grant us the serenity to accept the things we cannot change…"*

————

The day was gorgeous. It was one of those baby blue sky days, not the psychedelic candy blue nor the washed-out gray characteristics of Portland's typical rainy mornings. The clouds were puffs of radiant joy, ready to disperse into the wind. Lou watched them eddy, pure reflected rays dappled and swirling in the sky, until all that remained was that perfect shade of blue.

Lou turned her attention back toward the group of parents, children and their service dogs that were gathered outside of the Portland Guide Dog Association building in Troutdale. The scenery around them was picture-perfect. Which was more than they could ask for when taking these end-of-class pictures. It was typically raining, and they usually took them inside. This time had been an exception. Most were shading their eyes from the sunshine this morning. Tammy stood on Lou's right, alongside her fellow trainers, holding up her cellphone trying to get a good angle. "Alright, everybody. Group photo! Let's see some big smiles!"

Lou watched the far end of the line as Alice erupted into one of her beautiful full-faced smiles. The kind that always sent a shiver down her spine. The kind of smile that beat everybody else's by a long shot. And she couldn't help but smile too, when she saw Anna, whose own smile reflected that of her mother. They radiated. Stood out like diamonds, with the most handsome dog of the bunch. While Lou loved the satisfaction of another training class completed, at the same time it was bittersweet. Another group of great dogs were leaving the facility for their forever homes. This time, it was even harder than normal. For obvious reasons.

While many of the parents had already left, Lou was standing with Alice and Anna in the parking lot, helping her look over all her belongings that were packed tightly in her hire car. "Do you have everything? Do we need to make a quick stop at your parents?" Lou's stomach felt more unsettled than it had in a long time.

"I've got everything," Alice reassured her with a smile, helping Lou pack the last of Caspian's toys, stowing them away in a bag. "You can quit worrying." She leaned over to plant a kiss on Lou's cheek. Lou reached for her hand and squeezed it. "We're going to be okay, Lou. This is only temporary." The long distance. Alice was referring to the fact that they'd be three hours away from one another for a while. "We can see each other every other weekend. It's not that long of a drive. Don't worry."

"I might be there every weekend if you aren't careful," Lou joked, although her words were actually more serious than she'd been implying. The idea that Alice and Anna were leaving was terrifying her far more than she cared to admit, and she wasn't quite sure why.

"I wouldn't mind," Alice replied.

"Me either!" Anna piped up, and Lou laughed.

Meanwhile, Cooper was waiting patiently with his daughter Jesse and their dog Phil. He finally interrupted them, walking over to give Alice a brief hug. "Safe travels and stay in touch," Cooper said, smiling at her. When you come back to Portland to visit this one, give me a holler. Jesse would love to see Anna." Cooper's attention drifted to Lou. "It was nice to meet you, Lou. Thanks for the great class." He held out a hand.

Lou shook it, returning the smile and nodding. "Take care, Cooper."

Jesse and Anna were busy exchanging a hug. When they broke apart, Alice squatted down to say her goodbyes. Alice held on to Anna's shoulder as the father and daughter walked away with their dog. "I'm gonna miss her, Mama," Anna said, thoughtfully. Caspian seemed to sense her sadness, as he often did even with Lou, and licked at her face. Anna giggled.

Lou was busy looking back at Alice. Studying her gentle face and kind hazel eyes. Trying to remember all the little details about her in that moment, as she stood underneath the golden Portland sun. Why it felt like she was leaving for good, Lou had no idea. She hadn't realized how much she was staring until Alice turned her attention back toward her. "Are you okay?" Alice asked, brushing a strand of blonde hair out of her eyes.

"I'm okay," Lou reassured her. "Just a little sad you're both leaving. And I'm going to miss Caspian too." Lou hadn't even thought about the dog leaving, until that moment.

"I'll be in Portland the weekend after next, right?" Alice said, and Lou nodded. "Alright then. We'll make it work, okay? Don't worry. Promise me."

"I promise," Lou said, reaching out to brush the fingers of her right hand against Alice's face. She leaned into it, and Lou ran her thumb across the soft skin of her cheek. "Drive safe. Call me when you get in, so I know you all made it." Alice gave a teary smile, and Lou broke away from her, squatting down in front of Anna. The young girl seemed to notice Lou had joined her and turned her head so that she was facing in her direction. She was gripping onto Caspian's halter with one hand. "Hey Anna. Will you do me a favor?" Anna looked up at her. "Take good care of Caspian for me."

"I will," Anna replied, beaming at her. Her hand relaxed to move over the dog's neck and head, little fingers stroking his white fur. Lou placed her hands on either side of Caspian's face. Those blue eyes were locked on to Lou's, staring at her intensely.

"And you take care of Anna, alright?" Lou said to the dog, and he gave an affectionate soft bark, wagging his tail. Lou couldn't help but smile, before she wiped away a few stray tears from the corners of her eyes and stood back up. Caspian seemed to realize what was happening in that moment and nudged into her leg. Lou placed a hand on his head. "You're a good boy," she whispered.

When Lou's attention turned back on Alice, she noticed that her girlfriend was watching her. There was a hint of concern in her eyes, but Lou shrugged her off, still smiling. Anna interrupted them. "Are we going, Mama?"

"Okay, we should probably go. We have a long drive," Alice said, and Lou nodded. Everything was going to be okay. They'd see each other soon enough. "See you soon?"

"See you soon," Lou replied, leaning over to kiss her softly on the lips. When they broke away, Alice loaded the dog and her daughter in the car, and Lou followed alongside her as she hopped into the driver's side.

"Bye, Lou!" Anna called out from the backseat.

"Bye, Anna," Lou replied, before she patted the lip of the open window of the driver's door. Lou studied Alice for a moment before she turned away, wanting to go back into the building as quickly as possible. The wave of emotions washing over her was intense.

"Lou," Alice called out behind her, and when she turned back, she found Alice racing toward her. She threw her arms around Lou's neck and planted their lips back together again. Lou sighed, taking her in for a moment before Alice broke away. She was smiling. "I love you."

Lou's face, that had been trying to rein in her emotions, broke into a smile, washing away the sadness she'd been feeling in that moment. "I love you too," she breathed.

Chapter Eighteen

They watched their daughter.

Tears of joy drenched Alice Gray's cheeks that first day of kindergarten the following week after they'd left Portland. Bright, golden sunshine conjured the most brilliant of mosaics across the vinyl flooring as Anna and Caspian made their way over to a group of excited students gathered at a rainbow-colored table across the room. They came in flocks toward her and the dog, eager to meet them.

"Woah! You have a dog?" A little brown headed boy with coke bottle glasses approached them first. He stuck out his hand to pet Caspian, who nudged him gently. "He's so handsome. What's his name?"

"This is Caspian," Anna said, a smile stretched across her face. "I'm Anna."

"Hi Anna," another blonde headed girl said, standing beside the boy. She had a white and red cane in her hand, and Alice realized she must be partially sighted or blind like Anna was. The girl held out her hand in front of her and Caspian nudged his face toward it and licked at her fingers. She giggled happily. "I have a dog too. Her name is Pepper."

"Wanna come sit with us?" The boy asked, and Anna nodded enthusiastically.

"Follow, Caspian!" Anna instructed, and the dog followed alongside Anna's newfound friends. Alice placed a hand to her mouth, holding in a stifled cry. She felt Jeremy's arm wrap around her shoulder and offer a gentle squeeze. Alice's head fell onto the side of his face and Jeremy laughed, the two watching as Anna chatted with some other kids at the table while they all took turns petting the dog.

"I think she's going to be just fine, Al," Jeremy whispered into Alice's hair, and Alice couldn't help but laugh and nod in agreement. Relief overwhelmed her. She was still holding on to her daughter's jacket and backpack. Alice found her cubby, marked with her name in braille, and hung both on the rack situated inside. Her hand rested on the backpack for a moment, realizing what was about to happen. Anna was about to have her first day at school, alone, without her or Jeremy.

"I don't know if I can do this," Alice whispered, to no one in particular.

Jeremy placed his hands on her shoulders again. "You can do it. She'll be alright. You've got to let her take some risks, Al. It's just the nature of growing up." He was right. Alice knew he was, but it was still nerve-wracking regardless. When she turned back to look at Anna and saw her sitting in a chair alongside Caspian, she felt calmer. The dog was with her. Alice trusted Caspian more than she did most anything, including people. Her ex-husband seemed to read her mind. "Caspian's got her."

"I know," Alice took a deep breath and watched her daughter and the dog for a few moments more before she followed Jeremy out of the classroom. They walked down the cheerful yellow hallways, lined with artwork from the students. Jeremy and Alice had been on a waitlist for nearly a year to get into the small school for special needs children, and it had been worth the wait. She felt confident leaving Anna here.

"Feel better now?" Jeremy asked as he held the front door open for her, leading out into the round-about and the parking lot.

Alice nodded. "Much," she replied. In the round-about, a navy blue SUV was idling, and the sound of pop music played faintly. Jeremy and Alice made their way up to the car and found Hallie. She was a curvy short brunette, with thick curly brown hair and a bright cheerful smile. Alice had found her bubbly personality infectious since the moment they'd met. She was convinced she'd hate her at first. She was Jeremy's new love interest, after all. But she'd been far nicer and more perfect for Jeremy than she could have ever imagined. It was comfortable around her, and Alice had felt genuinely happy for both of them. "Hey, Hallie," Alice smiled, giving her a wave when she'd turned to look at them.

"Hey, Alice!" Hallie returned the wave and smiled. She tugged off her sunglasses momentarily so Alice could see her bright blue eyes that reminded her of Lou's. "Everything go okay with Anna?"

"She's great," Jeremy replied, as he opened the passenger side door to the car. Before he got in, he turned to offer Alice a hug, which she graciously accepted. Once they broke apart, he slid inside, shutting the door behind him.

"Do you want to get some breakfast with us?" Hallie offered. "We're going to the new diner down the street. They have killer eggs benedict." While Alice had been pondering on an excuse not to join them, when Hallie mentioned eggs benedict she hesitated. Jeremy must have mentioned her favorite breakfast food to her in passing at some point, but it flattered Alice that she'd remembered regardless. She was planning on heading to the high school to catch up on some work before the first of the fall semester started on Wednesday but it wouldn't hurt to have some company. "Sure," Alice smiled, hopping into the backseat.

———

The breeze blew a chill, announcing the coming of fall. The aroma of the tall grasses swaying around them, was an intoxicating perfume, and the starry night above was like a painting more sublime than any human could create. Twinkling lights, strung in the air by invisible strings. Alice had always loved Portland's night sky. They were far enough away from the city that the light pollution was minimal. Alice could make out the big dipper when she sought it out.

It had been two weeks since Alice had returned home to Seattle. Her head rustled against a soft gray quilt that had been stretched across a patch of grass. Twelve years ago, on this exact night, they'd been in this same spot. Looking up at this same sky. It was the night when Alice had given everything of herself to another person. The only other person in the world she had ever wanted to give herself to. And Lou had taken her virginity so delicately and intimately, that the rest of the world had fallen away, until it was just them. Much like it had been in these moments now.

Lou's mouth lit her skin on fire as it sucked on the hollow of her throat and made a wet trail down between Alice's pert breasts. They were flesh to flesh, having lost their clothes a long time ago. "Lou," Alice whispered into the air, as her focus was drawn to the beautiful redhead's bewitching blue eyes that stared up at her with a ravenous intensity. When Alice whispered her name, Lou knew exactly what she wanted. Their eyes locked together, and Lou straddled Alice's lap, and the other words she mumbled were smothered on Lou's lips as they came together, hard and searching. Alice tasted the sweetness of the remnants of the cheesecake they'd shared at the diner outside of town a few hours earlier. Lou moved her mouth, burying it in Alice's neck, finding that small spot near her shoulder that caused her entire body to quiver in delight.

When Lou looked at her again, it took Alice's breath away. It was easy for her to get lost in those eyes, and she was caught up in Lou's enthusiasm. Alice felt her fingers roaming up the cool flesh of Lou's hips, until they cupped her breasts, outlining them with her fingers as they swelled and tightened. Lou's breath grew ragged as Alice's fingers trailed down her stomach and danced across Lou's pelvic bone.

They twisted together, mouths crashing once more. Lou sucked Alice's bottom lip into her mouth, and she moaned in delight, her hips thrusting up into the redhead's body. Alice looked down, just as Lou made her way toward her breasts, her nipples budding pink and hard as she sucked and caressed them.Her body melted against

Lou's, succumbing to the whirlwind of pleasure she was feeling. Once Lou was satisfied with one nipple, she moved onto the other, while her free hand stroked down the length of Alice's stomach, drawing closer and closer to the wetness between her legs.

The impatience Alice was feeling grew to explosive proportions as Lou continued a trail of careful, methodical kisses from between her breasts, down to her pelvic bone. Alice propped herself up with her arms, watching. Lou's mouth and fingers burned her tingling skin as she breathed hot air above Alice's middle. She watched as Lou spread her open with her fingers, and then glanced up getting lost in her big luminous blue eyes. Just that look could send Alice crashing over the edge if she wanted. It was a hungry and eager look. Lou's tongue fell from her mouth, drawing a long stroke across Alice's clit, exploding every nerve inside Alice's body like fireworks.

Lou's name filled the late summer air in a gasp. Before she could think straight, Alice felt fingers fill her, juices flowing inside her like warm honey. The two found a tempo that sent Alice's head spinning, and within moments she was crying out for release, her pounding heart threatening to rip from her body. Every part of her quaked, and the feeling spread from the middle of her legs outward, in shivering waves, until she finally relaxed against the blanket.

Alice watched Lou as she trailed up her body, leaving kisses as she went. When Lou drew close enough, Alice's lips parted and she raised herself to meet her kiss, taking her mouth with a savage intensity. She didn't waste time, her hands exploring down the length of Lou, tracing around her breasts and running trails down her stomach. Fingers dipped between her legs and captured her clit between them.

A moan escaped Lou, and Alice felt her hips thrust forward, seeking her touch. Alice watched her as intently as she had moments earlier, as her fingers danced over her in a rhythmic way. Shivers of delight ripped through Lou, that Alice could feel down the length of them, as her fingers dipped inside the redhead, and then out again. A bright flare of desire sprang into Lou's eyes, as she pressed her lips to Alice's, just as her body shook ferociously. Lou gasped in Alice's mouth, over and over, as her hips pushed against Alice's thrusting fingers.

When Lou relaxed against her, they curled sideways onto the blanket, tangled around one another and breathing softly into the darkness of the world around them. Alice felt Lou's fingers stroking through her soft blonde hair, and the touch of her lips against her forehead. "Don't leave me," Lou whispered against her. "I don't think I could handle it again."

Alice broke away from her, staring at her eyes in the dim light of the sky above them. "Why would I leave you?" Her fingers drew against Lou's face, tracing the outline of her cheek. Lou didn't answer, just watched her. She'd gone distant. Alice moved forward to kiss her soft lips and smiled. "I promise," she said quietly. Lou offered a sad smile, looking far from comforted. Alice kept her hand against Lou's face, feeling the warmth in her cheeks. The rhythm of her breathing.

Lou was far away from that deserted field outside of Portland. Far away from Alice's embrace and the moment they'd just shared. And the hollow look in her eyes frightened Alice to a point that it sent a chill down her spine. "You're not alone," Alice reminded her, though her words seemed to have little effect on the mood that had swallowed Lou whole.

No, Alice wouldn't leave. Not again. Not from this. This was what she had needed all along. The thing that had been missing in her life for so long. It had been Lou. The one that had captivated her on the bus ride home from school all those years ago.

Her Lou.

Chapter Nineteen

They stood at the lone structure, reaching toward the sky. From outside the boarded windows, the shabby wood paneling and the pealing door that was bolted with iron rods, all looked scary and threatening enough to keep people out. It was enough to send Lou's nerves skyrocketing, more so than usual.

The weary double doors were painted racing green. Closed tight. There were holes, which upon further inspection looked like they were caused by bullets. The sight didn't ease Lou's mind, even though Detective Kennedy had told them the building was abandoned. Some part of Lou felt like she didn't want to go in alone with just Kennedy and Megan. But the building was empty and obsolete now. Just a hollow shell, covered in vines. The edges of the broken glass of the windows reminded her of a jagged coastline, the glass itself a gray-brown of settled dust. Around the brickwork was years of caked dirt.

It was clear this building had been unoccupied for a long time. There was nothing to fear.

Detective Kennedy stepped beside Lou. It was still early, barely any light in the sky. The days were getting shorter now that it was growing closer to winter. His black hair glistened in the glow of a nearby streetlamp. He pointed at the building. "You ladies ready to go get this done?"

While the building had been abandoned, there'd been reports that it was housing a puppy mill inside. As far as Lou understood it wasn't a front for a drug operation, but just a place to house a bunch of dogs. A terrible place that was making Lou angry just staring at it.

At least they'd be safe soon. Hopefully with new owners and homes.

The three headed inside, Rick taking the lead as he swung open the squeaky green door. Lou tried hard not to jump at the loud noise. Inside was as dusty and dank as the outside. There were few walls. It was mostly open, filled with dusty furniture that hadn't been used in a while.

From the far side of the building, Lou could hear the yelps and howls of dogs. They'd found the right spot. She couldn't tell how many there were, but it was obviously a lot. She, Kennedy, and Megan trekked across the building, heading toward the sound. Even knowing that the place was abandoned, it was still giving Lou the creeps, raising the hairs on the back of her neck with every step they took.

"There's something weird about this place," Megan whispered to Lou, who nodded in agreement. "I'm going to be glad to get out of here as soon as possible."

"Me too," Lou agreed. The two had seen their fair share of interesting places in the time she'd worked for the Humane Society, but this was right up there as one of the creepier ones. Especially for a place that was housing a puppy farm.

They rounded the corner into a room with windows that spanned the far wall. Most of them were broken, letting in the chilly Portland air. It definitely wasn't appropriate conditions for animals that was certain. On the opposite side of the windowed wall, crates and crates of dogs sat, of all varieties. Most of them were going crazy in their cages, the level of barking intensifying as they approached.

Megan and Lou set to work taking dogs from cages. Kennedy

helped wrangle them so that they could be taken out to the van. It would likely take two or three trips to get them all. Maybe even a trip to another shelter nearby. Lou wasn't sure the Humane Society would have enough room. Lou locked a pair of beagle pups in a crate inside of the van and headed back inside. Kennedy and Megan were busy putting dogs in the van as she headed back inside.

On the far side of the room, there were several crates that remained untouched. The room grew colder as Lou drew near. In one of the crates, a dog was lying completely on the floor. The way he looked reminded Lou oddly of Caspian all those years ago, when she'd first found him. Frightened and alone. Lou drew closer and could hear the low growl he was emitting.

In her hand, Lou only had a leash presently. Truthfully, she should have waited for the catchpole that Kennedy had with him. But Lou had felt more impatient and agitated lately, acting more reckless than she should have. She veered closer to the dog, who had not stopped growling. "It's okay buddy," Lou whispered, crouching down toward him. Trying not to maintain direct eye contact, so it didn't feel like Lou was threatening it in any way. "I'm just here to get you out of this place. We'll get you some place dry and warm. Wouldn't you like that?"

The growling stopped and the dog sat up, still watching here with a leery eye. Lou tried to convince herself to wait for Kennedy. He'd be back any second. But something urged her to approach anyway. She reached for the handle of the cage, pulling down on it lightly. Prepping the leash in her other hand so that she could wrap it around his neck when she was close enough.

He was just scared. That was all.

A blur of white charged at her before Lou could even get the cage open all the way. She fell back against the concrete floor of the building, her head hitting it with a loud 'thunk.' Lou had no time to think about her head, too focused on blocking her face as the dog pummeled on top of her, growling loudly again. She panicked, trying to push the mutt away. Fearing that at any moment it was going to attack her, and badly.

The world was growing blurry around her. Lou's anxiety was

overwhelming her senses, and her heart was beating so fast she knew that she was going to pass out at any minute. The last thing she remembered was Kennedy charging at the dog, and Megan wrapping the catchpole around its neck. Then Lou stopped thinking, and the world went black.

———

Lou's face fell against the cold tile of the bathroom, staring out into the hallway outside. The house was quiet. Dark. It was usually that way, but for the past few weeks it had felt even more so. She breathed in slow, shallow breaths while she tried to relax her body. It was early. Lou wasn't quite sure what time. The nightmares of the dog lunging at her had been keeping her up most nights, the past few days passing achingly slow. There was an intense throbbing radiating outward from the middle of her head and she felt immeasurably tired.

Somehow, Lou found the resolve to struggle her way off the floor and back to the safety of her bedroom. She had the urge to call Alice, but it was too early, and she was likely still sleeping. And even still, Lou wasn't sure Alice could even help her now. She'd begged Lou to come up to see her in Seattle at least a half-dozen times since the dog attack. But Lou had been convinced this was something she had to deal with on her own. When she glanced at the clock on her nightstand, she realized she only had a short while before Tammy would be by to pick her up for work. But she could close her eyes for a few minutes. Try to relax before she got ready.

When Lou woke again, it was because of a honking coming outside of her bedroom window. As soon as she'd managed to get to her feet, she looked outside the curtain seeing Tammy's blue van in the driveway. Lou waved a finger at her, telling her to wait. As quickly as she could, she threw on a T-shirt and jeans and pulled her hair up into a bun.

"You look a wreck," Tammy noted, as Lou slid into the passenger side of the van a few minutes later. She was still half asleep, barely able to keep her eyes open. Tammy's Goldendoodle,

Noodles, was laying stretched out on the floor behind them. When Lou looked back at him, it made her heart ache a little, and made her feel even more alone. Perhaps working with the new set of dogs would be good for her today. "Are you sure you feel up to working? You've had a stressful few weeks. I would understand if you need a few more days."

Lou finally looked back at Tammy. "I'm fine," she reassured her as they pulled back out of the driveway. Even with her mood, Lou somehow managed to make small talk with Tammy as they drove to Troutdale, while she admired the beautiful late summer day outside. She'd been cooped up in her house so much since Walter's death and Alice's return to Seattle, that she'd almost forgotten what it was like to admire the scenery around her.

"I've got you working with Stewart," Tammy said, breaking the silence that had formed as they pulled into the Portland Guide Dog Association parking lot. "He's a good dog. I think you'll like him a lot. Just do what you can today."

There was a surge of annoyance that washed through Lou, and before she could help herself, she snapped a reply. "I'm fine, Tammy." Then before Tammy could reply, she'd hopped out of the car without another word.

The new Labrador was waiting for Lou at the far end of the cages in the back room of the building. "Hey there, Stu," Lou said, grabbing a leash and a collar from the wall. Stewart had lived with a foster family for the past six months. A repeat family that often took their trainees. Stu's tail thumped noisily against the concrete flooring, tongue hanging out of his mouth. He gave an excited bark as Lou neared his kennel again. The other dogs had been retrieved already, so it was quiet outside of his barking.

The door barely opened, and Stu bounded into the aisle, still barking. Lou couldn't help but laugh at the dog's enthusiasm, turning in a circle to try to keep up with him. "Come here, Stu," Lou called out to him, taking a few steps toward him. "Come on, buddy. We've got stuff to work on today."

The dog bounded over to her at full speed. Before Lou could think, he'd jumped in her direction, and she panicked, falling backward onto the ground and shielding herself. An image of the scared white mutt at the abandoned building flashed in her mind, and Lou let out a terrified shout. Stewart immediately backed off, obviously startled. Lou backed her way to the wall of the building, trying desperately to take in air.

Anxiety was overwhelming her yet again, and she could feel dizziness taking over. Every fiber of her body was on fire with nerves. Before she knew it, the door had opened, and Tammy appeared in her peripheral. She fetched Stewart and leashed him. Then Lou watched as she came to sit beside her, a concerned look on her face. The Labrador sat on her opposite side, while Tammy placed a soft hand on Lou's shoulder. "Are you alright?"

"No," Lou said, her voice slightly shaking. She hadn't been alright. Not in weeks. Not since she'd seen Walter in that hospital room. Lou had felt terrified and alone. "I don't know what to do."

"Do you need to go to a meeting?" Tammy offered. Lou hadn't been to a meeting since Walter had died. She hadn't had the will to call the sponsor he'd suggested, Martha Winters, either. Instead she'd let herself spiral nearly out of control, and it felt like it was getting worse every day.

"No," Lou said, somewhat defiantly. "No—I—I just want to go home." She looked at Tammy, whose concern hadn't faded from her face. "I just need to go home. I shouldn't have come to work today. Not yet."

"Lou, you need to talk to someone," Tammy argued, her hand not leaving Lou's side. The gentle fingers roaming down felt like rain against her and had an instant calming effect. "I'm not telling you what to do, but I feel like it would really help you."

"I'm okay, Tammy," Lou argued. "I just need a few more days." But the truth was, she did need help. Far more than she cared to admit in that moment. Walter wasn't here to help her anymore. Lou was on her own. And that terrified her.

Chapter Twenty

Alice paced on the porch of the Craftsman house. It was pouring with rain outside. Anna was standing next to her with her hand wrapped around Caspian's halter. They'd been outside of the house for ten minutes. She'd called three times and banged on the door to no avail. Lou's yellow Volkswagen was parked in the driveway so supposedly she was home.

"Mama, are we going inside?" Anna asked, head tilting. Their impromptu visit had been at the insistence of Anna, who had thought it would be a good idea for Lou to be around Caspian. That the dog would somehow make her feel better than she'd been feeling.

Alice sighed, frustrated. "Stay here for a second, honey." She hated to leave Anna alone, but it was heavily raining out and she didn't want her daughter to trek through it if she didn't have to. "I'll be right back."

"Okay," Anna said, and Alice darted back into the torrent, and around the side of the house. Lou tended to lock the side door of the house, but Alice hoped on a prayer that for some reason she'd left it open. Sure enough, when she went to wiggle the handle, the door opened. It was dark and quiet inside.

"Lou?" Alice called, to which there was no answer. Maybe she'd somehow left the house. Alice wasn't quite sure where she would have gone. They'd stay until she got back, just to make sure she was safe. Alice went to the front door and opened it, letting her daughter and the dog inside. "Here, baby," Alice reached out for Anna, guiding her inside with Caspian's help.

Alice called for Caspian to follow her and led them both into Lou's living room, where a dark leather sofa sat against a wall. She let Anna sit, and Caspian came beside her obediently. Alice squatted down next to them. "Can you stay here for just a minute?"

"Where are you going?" Anna asked.

"Just to see if Lou is here," Alice promised her. "I'll be right back."

"Okay, Mama," Anna said, and clung onto Caspian's halter. "Stay, Caspian."

"Good boy," Alice said, scratching the dog on the head before she got back up to her feet. Just by how quiet the house was, Alice was certain Lou must have gone somewhere, but the fact that she hadn't answered her phone was still worrying her. "Lou?" Alice called, walking down the hallway.

There was a noise from the bedroom nearby. For a minute, it sent her heart fluttering, but eventually she moved straight toward the door, opening it. Inside, Lou was curled up in the bed. Alice couldn't tell if she was asleep or not. "Lou?" Alice whispered into the darkness. The body on the bed didn't move, and Alice felt a wave of panic as she rushed into the room. She landed on the edge of the bed, finding Lou buried beneath a mess of covers and pillows. "Lou!" Alice gave her a violent shake, and she heard Lou gasp in surprise, her eyes fluttering open.

The thudding in her heart wouldn't calm. "Jesus, Lou. You scared me."

"Alice?" Lou stared up at her with hazy eyes. "What time is it?"

"It's dinner time," Alice said, looking at the clock on her night-stand that read a little after six. "I told you Anna and I were coming for a visit after I got off work, remember? Anna wanted to come and see you with Caspian. She thought it would do you good." Lou sat up wobbly in bed. Alice hadn't talked to her since early that morning, and even then, it had been brief. Something was off about her. "Are you okay?"

Lou blinked, turning her attention back to Alice. "Just sleepy."

"Did you go to work today?" Alice asked her, as she watched Lou try to get herself out of bed. Judging by her appearance, Alice would have guessed Lou hadn't. "Lou."

Surprisingly, Lou shot back an answer quickly. "I'm fine Alice." Her tone was short. Alice didn't like it at all. "Can you give me a second?"

Alice got up to leave, feeling frustrated. The minute she reached the door, she turned back to Lou. "Lou, you haven't been—I mean, you didn't take anything—" Alice's voice trailed off when Lou's head snapped up looking at her. She looked panicked and at the same time angry, but Lou couldn't tell what it was from.

"Jesus, Alice. Why would you even say that?" Lou's voice had risen slightly.

Alice motioned for Lou to quiet her voice, because of Anna. "You're just acting weird," Alice argued at the doorway. She tried to stay calm. "I'm worried is all."

"I told you, I'm fine," Lou said, still sounding agitated. Alice didn't press her further, heading back down the hallway and leaving Lou alone. She met Anna in the living room with Caspian.

"Mama?" Anna asked, as Alice rounded the corner.

"Yes, baby?" Alice said, sitting down on the couch beside her, letting out a long breath of air. She wasn't quite sure what to do. Alice certainly didn't want Anna around Lou the way she was. And she had no way of knowing what was wrong if Lou wasn't going to talk to her.

"Is Lou okay?" Anna's voice interrupted Alice's racing thoughts.

"She's okay," Alice lied, trying her best to maintain her composure. Lou certainly wasn't okay, but there was no need to worry Anna. "In fact, I think we're going to let her rest for a little while. I think she's kind of tired." Alice decided that they'd go to her parents for a bit. Maybe she'd come back later without Anna to make sure

Lou was alright. She didn't need to be here now. "Come on, we'll go see what grandma and grandpa are up to."

Alice helped her daughter up from the couch and started to head toward the door, letting Caspian lead. The moment she'd reached it, she heard a commotion down the hallway. Alice turned just in time to see Lou stumbling. There was something wrong. She looked nothing like herself. Skinnier than normal, hair in disarray. There were dark circles under her eyes, and she looked so out of it that it was a wonder she was standing upright. Alice feared the worst in that moment. Worried that Lou had done something she shouldn't.

And she wasn't about to expose her daughter to it.

"Not now, Lou," Alice warned her, before Lou had an opportunity to speak. "I'm going to take Anna home and then I'll come back later, and we can talk."

"Lou?" Anna piped up and turned in the direction of the noise in the hallway. Alice tugged at her daughter, trying to get her to head over to the door.

"Hi, Anna," Lou said, in a quiet and steady voice. At least as steady as she could make it given the circumstances. Her eyes had shifted from Alice's daughter to the dog and then back again.

"Are you okay?" Anna asked, holding onto Caspian's halter. "Mama says you're tired."

Lou let out a laugh, which startled Lou. While part of her felt annoyed at Lou's nonchalance of the situation, another part of her was still worried that something was terribly wrong. "I've just been a little stressed out lately," Lou said.

"Is it because your friend died?" Anna asked, without any reservation.

"Come on, Anna," Alice interrupted her, tugging her again toward the door. "Lou, I'll be back in a little bit."

Lou ignored her, still looking at Anna. "Yeah, it's because of my friend." Alice paused, turning to look at Lou again. "And the dog that attacked me a few weeks ago. It scared me."

"I get scared sometimes too," Anna piped up. "Like when I have to go to the doctor. You know what Mama always tells me when I get scared?"

Lou paused, shook her head, and then realized she needed to speak. "No. What does she tell you?"

"Mama says you have to stand up to fear," Anna said, matter-of-factly. "Mama says if you know you're scared, you won't be scared anymore. It's magic."

Lou laughed again, and this time it sounded more natural. A genuine laugh. And when Alice looked at her, her lips had curled upward just a fraction. "Magic, huh?"

"Uh huh," Anna agreed.

"Okay, sweetheart," Alice said, interrupting them again. "Let's get you to grandma and grandpas. Maybe we can come visit Lou tomorrow?"

"Okay," Anna said. "Bye, Lou!"

"Bye, Anna," Lou replied. Alice glanced at her one last time before she turned toward the door. Anna stopped abruptly before they'd made their way out of the house and turned back in the opposite direction.

"Lou?" Anna said, pipping up again. Lou walked a few paces to the door.

"Mm?"

"It's okay to be scared."

———

It was close to nine. Alice wasn't quite sure if Lou would still be up, but she went back to the house anyway. The front porch light was on as she turned into the driveway. It had been a nice night out, so she'd decided to walk. Alice wrapped her jacket around her as she stood in front of the door. The minute she reached it, she knocked.

Lou must have been close by. The door opened only a few seconds later and Alice could tell she'd cleaned herself up a little. Lou's hair was still damp but pulled up in a bun on top of her head. She was wearing an oversized University of Oregon sweatshirt, and a pair of sweatpants. Her eyes were a little puffy, like she'd been crying.

Truthfully, she still looked bad. Worse than Alice had seen her since they'd been together all those years ago. "Are you going to tell me what's going on?" Lou didn't answer, instead stepping out of the doorway and inviting her inside. Alice made her way across the room to the couch and sat down. Lou followed, sitting beside her. They both turned to face one another, but Alice noticed that Lou couldn't look at her directly. "Please talk to me."

"I can't talk to you," Lou said, an unreadable look stretched across her face. Alice couldn't tell if she was angry or what she was feeling. "You don't understand. You can't understand. I'm alone, Alice. I'm all alone. Ever since Walter died…"

Alice thought she would feel offended by Lou's sudden outburst but instead she felt compassion. "Lou, you aren't alone. I'm here, okay? I'm here for you." She reached out for Lou's hand, but Lou pulled away at the last second. "You need to get some help. You're clearly not yourself, and I think it would be good for you to talk to someone."

"I don't need to talk to someone," Lou snapped, getting to her feet. "I need Walter. But he's not here anymore. I'm all alone." There were tears streaming down her face, but Alice sat helpless, watching as Lou paced the floor a panic-ridden mess. "And I can't tell you how much I need relief right now. And not an appropriate kind of relief."

"Then let's get you some," Alice argued. "We'll make you an appointment with the doctor. Just because they want to give you medicine, doesn't mean it has to be addictive, Lou. You just have to be patient and brave and try it."

"No," Lou said defiantly.

"So, you're just going to sit here and be miserable?" Alice argued. "And fall apart?"

"I guess so," Lou replied, unable to look at her then. Instead she was looking at the floor, and it seemed as though she was fighting terribly hard to hold back tears. "I can figure it out on my own."

"Please get some help, Lou. I'm begging you." Alice tried to reach for her hand again that was only a foot or so away, but Lou pulled away. "Please." She could hear her own voice cracking, getting emotional.

"I'll figure it out, Alice," Lou argued again. "Just stay out of it."

A surge of frustration overwhelmed Alice then. She wasn't quite sure what to do. How to help Lou in this moment, or even if she was willing to accept help. "Well, I can't sit idly by while you destroy yourself, Lou. I won't do it. I have my daughter to think of." Alice watched Lou continue to pace the floor, seeming to grow more and more frustrated by the second. Like she would implode at any moment into a million pieces. It terrified her. She wanted desperately to help her in any way she could, but she was feeling rather helpless in that moment. "I can't watch you fall apart and not want to help yourself."

Their eyes met and Alice's blood went cold when she saw Lou's eyes turn hard and distant. Unsure if she was angry or upset, or a little bit of everything. "Then I guess you should leave," Lou said, defiantly. "You're good at that."

Pain shot through her at Lou's words. Was she really bringing up something that happened eight and a half years ago? Something that had plagued Alice with guilt ever since. A surge of anger washed over her and Alice got to her feet, glaring at Lou. Even if she was hurting, even if something was wrong, Alice couldn't help her if she was being unreasonable. She got to her feet, walking around Lou and toward the door. When she reached back, she turned to look over her shoulder. Defiant blue eyes were watching her, and while they had softened, her face remained hard and stubborn. "I love you, Lou. And I'm sorry you're hurting," Alice said simply. "But if you want Anna and me to be a part of your future, you need to learn to trust me again. And find a way to let yourself heal."

———

The ancient mullioned windows set the dark myrtle wood flooring of the classroom ablaze with a checkerboard of early fall sunlight. It had been a week since Lou and Alice had spoken to one another and since then, the first days of school had started. Alice's attention drew back to her students that had been finishing a reading during the class period. *Fahrenheit 451*. Ray Bradbury had always been a favorite of Alice's. Perhaps it was his infectious joy for his craft that had inspired her as a teacher, hoping it would rub off on her students.

"Alright," Alice said, looking out at the class of thirty students, scanning across the room. Heads popped up and turned their focus toward her. "Let's talk a little about the portion you just read. Can anyone tell me what they think the central theme of *Fahrenheit 451* might be?"

Hands rose across the room and Alice picked one at random. A young and sprightly girl, with eager brown eyes that were cased under a pair of square glasses. "It's talking about the conflict between freedom of thought and censorship? People gave up reading and books, and they don't feel oppressed or censored?"

"Exactly," Alice turned to scribble across the whiteboard behind her. 'Censorship vs. Freedom of Thought.' Once she'd finished, she turned back facing the class. "What sort of factors do you think contributed to why books are banned in the future?"

A hand shot up. This time it was a brunette boy in the front row, next to the eager eyed girl. Alice pointed at him. "The popularity of competing forms of entertainment. It seemed like Bradbury was alluding to the idea that there was too much distraction. Too many overwhelming published materials."

"Also, envy." The girl noted.

Alice turned her attention to her, raising a curious brow. "What do you mean?"

"Well," the girl stated, looking down at her textbook briefly. "People don't like to feel inferior to those that have read more than they have. And people don't like reading about things that offend them."

"Interesting thought," Alice agreed, and scribbled across the whiteboard again. When she turned back toward the class, she glanced up at the clock on the wall, realizing the class was almost over for the day. "Okay. For your homework assignment, I want you to write a short two-page essay about one of those themes. Expand on what that theme means in interpreting Bradbury's work. It doesn't have to be a super clean essay. I just want you to free-write." The bell rang, and students immediately started to pack away their things. "Bring in your papers next week and we'll talk about it. Have a good day."

The class left without any questions that day. Instead, Alice was left alone in an empty classroom for an hour, free to do what she wanted with her time. She already had papers to grade from her earlier senior English class. A large stack sat on one side of her desk. She'd been avoiding them all morning, but finally decided to get on with it. As soon as she sat down, her phone buzzed on the desk. Alice picked it up frantically, hoping every time it rang it was Lou. Disappointed, she saw Jeremy's number stretched across the screen. He very rarely called her during the school day, but he'd been taking Anna to school late that morning after a doctor's appointment.

"Hello?" Alice answered, feeling a weird stirring in her stomach.

"Alice," the voice on the other end of the phone was deathly serious and quiet. The sound of it sent a chill racing down Alice's spine. "Something's happened to Caspian."

Chapter Twenty-One

Lou loved the sky before a thunderstorm. The silver hues, like molten silver, swirling in steady and radiant ripples. The grays of every shade and depth, and the way the atmosphere was so subtly electric, alive with excitement of what was to come.

Just as a drop of crystal-clear water appeared on her arm, Lou looked up at the sky. The rain was something that usually stopped her thoughts from buzzing and calmed her. The heavy drops of liquid hitting the pavement behind her, creating a melancholic song. Lou waited for the rain to wash away the misery she'd been feeling for weeks now, standing under the long sweeping branches of an oak tree, her gaze burning into the headstone that was in front of her.

Walter J. Harris.

The tears falling down Lou's face blended with the soft rain that was falling, so she couldn't tell which was which. She squatted down, resting her hand on top of the stone, feeling its grainy texture beneath her fingertips. A sigh escaped her.

"I miss you," she said, to no one in particular. Perhaps she was talking to Walter. Maybe she was just talking to herself. Lou didn't know anymore. She only knew she was tired of feeling alone, especially when she was in such desperate need. "I wish you were here."

The sound of raindrops hitting the tops of stone and dancing on the leaves of the trees grew louder. It was starting to become harder to see through the downpour, and it had gotten significantly colder, but Lou stood there anyway. "I don't know what to do, Walty." Lou hadn't known what to do for almost two weeks now. She hadn't been able to function. It had taken everything in her power not to succumb to every desire to ease her anxiety and her pain.

So, in an hour of desperate need, she turned to the one person who knew her well. "I don't think I'm going to make it. I keep pushing people away. I keep failing, even when I'm trying not to."

Lou remembered the first time she'd seen Walter at a Narcotics Anonymous meeting. It had been raining that evening too, just like it was today, which wasn't unusual for Portland. She'd been standing in the doorway leading into the basement of the church, a nervous wreck. Watching the group of people gathered, chatting amongst themselves. Lou had been certain she wouldn't be able to go to the meeting. That somehow, she'd walk out.

But then there had been a friendly hand on her shoulder. It had taken Lou by surprise, and she'd nearly jumped out of her skin. "They aren't going to bite ya kid," Walter had said, his signature smile stretched across his lips. That familiar twinkle in his eye when he spoke. Somehow, his presence had changed everything about that moment. Lou had felt welcome. At peace. She gathered her strength and followed him as he made his way inside the room.

They sat together the entire night, and at the meeting Walter scrawled his cell number on the back of a napkin. "If you need to talk," he'd said. "I'm around."

He had been around for eight years and had filled the empty hole in her life since Alice had left. Somehow, she'd made it through to the other side. Now, Alice was back, and Walter was gone, and still there was something missing inside her. She'd fought for eight years to have her life back to normal, and just when it seemed to be heading that way, it had spiraled into chaos again.

And now Alice was gone again, too. Lou was completely alone. "What am I supposed to do, Walty?" Lou asked again, to the air. Raindrops washed her face and were forming a puddle in the mud at her feet. "What am I supposed to do?" Lou stuffed her hands inside of her green jacket, and her fingers wrapped around a slip of paper. She pulled it out, unfolding it and stared down at the screwed up note. The name Martha Winters was scratched out on top of the page, along with a telephone number, in Walter's scribbly handwriting. Lou's new sponsor that Walter had found.

A laugh, mixed with a brief hint of a cry escaped Lou, and she smiled at the tombstone, shaking her head. She stared at the paper again and folded it back in her hand. Patted the tombstone goodbye and gave it one last glance before she trekked back to her car. She could feel her phone vibrating in her pocket as she started the engine. When she pulled it out, Alice's name was stretched across the screen. It had been a week since they'd last talked. Lou hadn't had the courage to call her before then. She swallowed and put the phone to her ear.

"Lou," Alice was sobbing on the other end of the line. She mumbled something in between her tears, but Lou couldn't make it out.

"Alice, you need to take a breath," Lou said calmly, though she could feel her anxiety heightening at the sound of Alice's heaving sobs. "Tell me what's going on."

"It's Caspian," Lou had managed to make out what Alice said this time, through the sobbing heaving cries on the other end of the phone. "Lou, please come to Seattle."

———

I t was the kind of early autumn day that would usually have Lou's spirits soaring beyond the colorful boughs above her, driving down the side streets on the outskirts of Seattle. The brilliant shafts of sunlight caressed the carpet of red and gold, and each breath of fresh air she took out the rolled down window filled her up with a sense of life that almost made her want to shout out loud, just to hear her voice amidst the trees. Or maybe from the nerves that were racing through her, Lou wasn't quite sure.

Even with the uncertainty that lay ahead, Lou was calmer than she'd been in years. Even though her hands were clammy, and her heart was far from steady, she felt stronger than she'd known herself to be in a very long time. Lou turned into the parking lot of the veterinary hospital and found a familiar blonde headed woman pacing the sidewalk outside. She'd called Alice a half hour ago to let her know she was nearing Seattle. Lou wondered if she'd been standing outside the entire time waiting. As soon as the bumblebee yellow Beatle pulled into the parking spot, Alice raced for Lou's car.

It wasn't even a second after Lou got out that Alice had wrung her arms around her neck. Alice very rarely was one to cry, usually the stronger of the two, but this time Lou could feel her weeping softly into Lou's shoulder. They hugged tightly, and Lou breathed in the freshness of the blue cardigan she was wearing, with a matching blue and white dress. Felt the welcoming and loving touch of the woman she loved so dearly.

And Lou knew in that moment, whatever Alice needed, she'd give it to her, without any shadow of a doubt. "What happened?" Lou asked, pulling away from her finally to meet those eyes, a mixture of autumn tones and so light and delicate.

"Jeremy said Anna tripped in the road walking up to school, and Caspian darted in front of an oncoming car——" Alice could hardly get the words out. The image of Caspian moving to protect Anna reminded Lou of the time when Caspian had saved her from the dog attack so many years ago. She'd known from the moment that they'd met that he'd be a good dog. "He's still in surgery. He was hurt pretty badly——"

"Let's go inside," Lou suggested, reaching to wrap Alice's hand in her own.

"I'm glad you're here," Alice said, her eyes having grown red and puffy. Despite her appearance, Lou thought she was the most beautiful thing she'd ever seen. And even with her panic and anxiety, Lou still felt a sense of calm. Like she was supposed to be the one to keep it all together in these moments. That it was her job to stay strong for all of them.

"Me too," Lou said, holding open the front door for her.

Inside, Alice's ex-husband Jeremy, his girlfriend Hallie, who Lou had never met, and Anna sat in the waiting room. Jeremy was busy consoling his daughter, who had her arms wrapped around his neck and sat in his lap. When Alice and Lou came to join them, Anna's attention turned toward the approaching footsteps.

"Mama?" Anna asked, and Alice reached out to touch her daughter's arm.

"Lou's here," Alice said, turning back to look at Lou briefly.

"Hi Anna," Lou said, and Anna shifted her position in her father's lap and turned her head in the direction of Lou's voice. "I'm glad you're okay."

"Caspian's hurt," Anna said, and Lou could tell by the way she was speaking that she was scared and nervous. Lou got up from her seat again, coming to kneel in front of Anna, who was still situated in Jeremy's lap. She reached out a hand to run it through the young girl's wispy blonde hair that looked so much like her mother's. "I'm sorry. I didn't mean to get him hurt."

"You remember what you told me a few weeks ago," Lou said, calmly, letting her fingers stroke the top of Anna's head. "About what your mom says when you're scared?"

"Mhm," Anna replied, sniffing loudly.

"What did you tell me?"

Anna breathed before she spoke. "That—that if you say you're scared, it won't be so scary." Anna shifted on her father's lap, still tilting her head over to listen to Lou.

"Are you scared?" Lou asked her, studying the little girl's sweet sad face, and glancing at Alice briefly, who, like Jeremy, had her full attention on Lou in that moment. Anna nodded.

"Well me too," Lou said, reaching down to wrap her hand over Anna's small one. "But what else did you tell me?" Anna hesitated, clearly unsure at this point what Lou meant, so she continued. "That it's okay to be scared." The little girl smiled somewhat, but before she could reply, there was the sound of footsteps clipping along the floor. When Lou turned her head in the direction of the sound, there was an older curly brown-haired woman headed toward them wearing a pair of scrubs.

Alice immediately got to her feet, greeting the woman as she stopped in front of the group. She instinctively reached for Lou's hand, and Lou held onto her as they waited for the woman to speak. "You must be Caspian's family," she said, her eyes glancing over each of them individually. "We've just got done with the surgery. He has a long recovery ahead of him, but he's going to be okay."

An air of relief seemed to pass through the group. "He's going to be okay?" Anna repeated, in a somewhat squeaky sounding tone.

"He's going to be okay, baby," Alice said, her voice equally as squeaky and emotional. There were silent tears running down her face, and Lou squeezed her hand softly to comfort her.

"You want to go see him?" Jeremy asked Anna, who nodded. He and his girlfriend got to their feet with the young girl.

"I need a minute," Lou said, clearing her throat. She tugged Alice to the side of the group and watched as the veterinarian led the three of them out of the room and into the back of the building where Caspain was in recovery. Meanwhile, Lou was still holding onto Alice's hand. When they were alone together in the waiting area, her attention turned on Alice again. "Alice—"

"You don't need to say anything," Alice said, placing a finger to her lips. Lou reached for her hand, entangling it with her own and pulling it down to waist height. Before Alice could speak another word, Lou moved her mouth over Alice's, devouring its softness. The kiss sang through her, top to bottom, setting her aflame.

When they finally broke apart, Lou was smiling. "I'm going to get help," she promised Alice. "I'm going to go talk to someone. Next week. I'll make an appointment. I'll start going to meetings again—" Alice's face broke whilst Lou was speaking, nodding through all of it. "I just… I need you to promise me one thing."

"Anything," Alice said quietly, hands still wrapped tightly in Lou's own.

"Promise me you'll stay."

Chapter Twenty-Two

One year later…

The weather at Rooster Rock Park was the kind that felt like a kiss of summer without the fiery heat of noon time in August. The grass was a soft green that almost had a hint of blue, and in the sky was enough pristine white clouds to show how beautiful it was, how perfect. Earthy toned trees, whose leaves were all different shades of fall colors, hung above them. The air was tangy and sweet, almost as fresh as an apple from an orchard.

Underneath the tent in front of her, all her family and friends sat. For years, Lou Pearson had felt so alone in the world. Yet here she was, on the happiest day of her life, surrounded by more people she called family than she ever thought possible. Lou watched them as she walked beside her brother Stephen, with her arm wrapped around his.

"Congratulations," her brother whispered once they'd stopped. He leaned inward to kiss Lou softly on the cheek and then sat down in the front row next to Kelly and Rebecca. Tammy was standing waiting for her at the front. It had been a last-minute decision on Alice and Lou's part to have Lou's best friend and co-worker officiate the ceremony, but Lou couldn't have imagined a better person to do it.

"Nervous?" Tammy whispered, having leaned into Lou. Lou smiled, realizing that the fears and anxieties that had plagued her for years had gotten so much better. Ever since she'd started going to therapy and taking medication, ever since she'd met up with Martha Winters and kept up with her NA meetings… Lou never dreamed her life would be as calm as it was now. While it wasn't perfect by any means, it was better than she could have ever imagined it.

And today, it was about to become even more so.

In the aisle, Alice watched as the beautiful white German Shepherd, adorned in a fancy black bowtie, walked straight over to her. At his side walked Anna, the wispy blonde-haired girl that Lou had fallen in love with as much as her mother. She was smiling brightly, as they walked together, and when they reached Lou's side, Lou reached down to run her fingers over Caspian's head in gratitude, while she held on to Anna's shoulder.

"Lou," Anna said in a whisper, her head tilting up.

"Yeah?" Lou replied, looking down at her.

"I'm glad you're going to be in our family," Anna said, matter-of-factly, and her words brought a smile so bright to Lou's face that she thought it might tear it in half.

"I'm glad too," Lou replied. The music was playing again, and Lou looked up, just in time to see the beautiful blonde head of Alice turn into the aisle. She hadn't seen Alice Gray in her dress. Not before this moment. It was a simple design, white with floral accents, not even a proper wedding dress really, but it matched Alice perfectly in every way. It brought out the swirl of colors in her eyes that Lou loved so much. Honestly, Lou couldn't have cared less what she was wearing in that moment, being far too captivated by the smile that was stretched across her face. A smile that she knew for certain they were both sharing.

When Alice reached her side, Lou couldn't help but lean in to kiss her. "You look nice," Alice whispered to her, admiring the suit pants and vest Lou had chosen to wear, in lieu of a dress. Alice had wanted her to be comfortable, after all. "Are you ready?"

Lou had waited nearly a decade for this moment. There was no question in her mind. "Always."

L aughter filled her ears. Lou looked upon the gazebo, filled with her family and closest friends at their low-key reception. Stephen was busy at the grill, making a spread of barbequed food, while Kelly, James, Lily and Betty worked on preparing side dishes, with the help of Tammy, Megan, and Rick Kennedy. Across the way, Cooper's daughter Jesse, Rebecca and Anna were throwing a stick for Caspian, Phil, Noodles and Benji, while Cooper watched them from a bench. Lou stood mesmerized by the happy animals for a minute, the kids laughing happily. She felt a hand fall into her own and turned to see Alice standing beside her.

"Do you feel married yet?" Alice asked her, and Lou laughed in response.

"I always felt like I belonged to you, even when we weren't married," Lou said, glancing at her. "But I'm glad we are. I love you so much."

"Me too," Alice agreed, smiling down at the gold band that now adorned her finger.

"CASPIAN!" Rebecca shouted, and Lou's attention turned back in the direction of the dogs and kids. The white German Shepherd had disappeared over the hill, out of sight.

"You'd better go get him," Alice pointed at the field. Lou took off in a hurry, around the picnic tables and out into the dewy grass. The hill dipped into a brush, where Lou assumed the dog had disappeared into. Lou let out a whistle and waited.

"Caspian! Come on loonie!" Lou stood frustrated, waiting for the dog to appear.

There was a yelp, and a hiss, and Lou's blood ran cold. Bounding from the brush, Caspian appeared, tail tucked between his legs as he scampered as fast as his legs could carry him toward Lou. Lou stood frozen for a moment, unsure of how to react.

That was until she saw the black and white fur, running full speed after the dog.

"Caspian!" Lou shouted, as the dog whizzed by her. The skunk was gaining speed on them. Lou turned, darting in the same direction as the dog. Straight back over to her family at the picnic tables. Her family and friends laughing as she and the dog ran full speed ahead, happiness surrounding her as she ran toward their love.

"Watch out!!"

Printed in Great Britain
by Amazon

54264758R00111